Doing the Impossible

tk ralya

PublishAmerica
Baltimore

First printing

At the specific preference of the author, PublishAmerica allowed this work to remain exactly as the author intended, verbatim, without editorial input.

ISBN: 1-4241-1623-6
PUBLISHED BY PUBLISHAMERICA, LLLP
www.publishamerica.com
Baltimore

Printed in the United States of America

to my mother, Ruth Ralya, for helping me grow up
and my two daughters, Angie and Aubrey,
who continue to bless my life every day

Chapter One

Megan grabbed Ashley's arm as she passed her in the hall. "Will you look for me? I can't stand the suspense."

"Look at what?" asked Ashley, frowning.

"The results of the play tryouts are posted outside Ms. Hillman's room."

"So? Go see what part you got."

"I can't! Will you look for me?"

By this time, Brittany had come up beside them.

"Oh, Megan, stop being so dramatic. You know you probably got the lead."

"But that's just it! What if everyone expects me to get the lead, but I didn't?" Her voice fell to a whisper. "I couldn't bear it."

"Oh, for heaven's sake!" replied Brittany unsympathetically, but Ashley knew Megan well enough to know that the overly dramatic exterior was a facade, and the poor girl really was nervous.

"Wait here," she said, and she made her way through the crowd outside the drama classroom. In her effort to see the results, she tried to squeeze between two boys who were taller than she was, and ended up being smashed into David Weston. "Hey, watch out!" he grumbled. "What are you doing here anyway? Ms. Hillman's too smart to give a part to someone who looks like you!"

Ashley felt her cheeks burn, but she made no reply. As soon as she was close enough to confirm that Megan had, indeed, gotten the lead, she slipped out of the crowd as invisibly as she could.

"You got the lead!" she called to Megan when she was still several feet away, trying to be as cheerful as she could.

Megan clenched her fist and pulled it towards her in a gesture to emphasize her "Yesssssss!" Then she looked anxiously to Ashley again. "Who got the male lead?"

"Kevin Bradley. But don't ask about any others, I didn't memorize the whole thing."

"You just knew she'd want to know that one! Kevin Bradley. Oh, brother," put in Brittany, "she'll be in love by tomorrow."

"You're just jealous," replied Megan.

"No way. I've heard about the rehearsals you drama people have. Things get pretty friendly from what I hear."

"We're just all really good friends. It's no big deal."

Ashley was getting uncomfortable. She hated when Megan and Brittany went after each other.

"When do rehearsals start?" she asked, trying to divert the conversation.

"Next week, I think."

"Oh. That's nice. Well, I guess I'd better go. The bus will be leaving soon."

"Why don't you have your mom drive you like everybody else instead of riding that stupid bus?"

"Oh, Megan," Brittany said with exasperation, "leave her alone. Not everybody has a mom who has nothing better to do than drive her kids around."

Ashley could see that they were determined to argue, so she made a quick escape, calling "Bye!" as she ran down the hall. Once on the bus, she concentrated on staring at some imaginary object outside the window. Maybe if she stared hard enough, she could keep the tears from coming. After all, it wasn't her fault she was ugly, but somehow knowing it when you look in the mirror is not the same as having someone else point it out.

She got off the bus and walked to the front of the house just as she saw her mother drive into the garage in back. Rats! She had hoped to have time to herself before having to deal with her mother. Her mom always seemed to know when something was bothering her, and she didn't feel like talking about it right now.

"Hi, Honey! How was your day?" her mom called from the back of the house.

"Fine. Anything happen at work today?"

"Same old stuff, now how 'bout you tell me what happened today?"

"What are you talking about?"

Her mom walked into the living room where Ashley had dumped her book bag.

"Ashley, I've known you for all of your fifteen years, and every time you don't want to talk about something, you change the subject. You don't ask me about my day unless you want to keep me from talkin' about yours. Now come on, let's have it."

Ashley sighed and rolled her eyes up towards the ceiling.

"It was no big deal."

7

"You sound like Megan."

Her mother just kept looking at her, so she knew she had to continue.

"Megan got the lead in the play."

"So?"

"So she was too nervous to look and asked me to look for her." Ashley was talking faster now in an effort to get it over with. "And when I went over to look at the list, a boy asked me what I was doing there because I was obviously too ugly to be in a play. There! Are you satisfied?"

"Oh, Honey, that's awful! What did you say to him?"

"Nothing."

"Well, that's probably best. There's not much you can say to someone who is so bad-mannered as to say such a thing."

"It's the truth."

"Don't be ridiculous! Of course it's not the truth! You may not be a knockout, but you have a very pleasant face, and I wouldn't exchange you for the most beautiful girl in the world. There are more important things in life."

The words had been said so many times, Ashley knew them by heart. When she was younger, they had given her some degree of comfort, but now they were too well-worn to work.

As she turned to go upstairs, she said, "I'm going to start my homework now. We have a big English assignment."

"Don't you think some fresh air would do you some good first?"

Ashley smiled. Her mother thought fresh air could cure about anything. "Maybe later, when I need a break."

She picked up her book bag and headed up the stairs. In her room, however, the atmosphere was no more conducive to work than it would have been downstairs with her mother watching her with one eye. She decided to write in her diary to get her gloomy thoughts out of her mind so it could be clear for studying.

September 16
'Dear Diary,
Today David Weston called me ugly. Well, not in so many words, I suppose, but I knew what he meant. Would it really have been such a big deal for God to have given me a face worth looking at? Brittany says I'm lucky because I'm not overweight like she is, but I don't think so. At least her face is pretty, and she has brains, too. If she's feeling bad about how she looks, she can feel better by looking at her report card. She's never going to have to worry about getting into college! They'll probably pay her to go to their school!

I'll be lucky to get in. When I look at my report card, all I see are C's and maybe a couple B's if I'm lucky, and that's with trying my hardest. God knows what would happen if I quit trying! It's not fair! When God was giving out gifts, He passed me by...

Oh well...this kind of talk doesn't do any good, and it certainly won't help me get my English done. Mom likes to show me the quote where Bahá'u'lláh says each child is a mine rich in gems. How does it go? "Regard man as a mine rich in gems of inestimable value. Education can, alone, cause it to reveal its treasures, and enable mankind to benefit therefrom."

Personally, I think I got rock salt. I guess I can't call Bahá'u'lláh wrong, but my report card sure doesn't sparkle! My gems must be buried way down deep where I can't see them.

Whatever...

I need to go become a "brilliant" literary critic...
—Ashley

9

Chapter Two

Mr. Jameson had already taken roll in Bahá'í school when Megan dragged herself into the classroom. As she plopped down beside Brittany and Ashley, Brittany asked, "Late night?"

"Melissa had a slumber party last night, but Mom and Dad wouldn't let me skip Bahá'í school." She laid her head down on her arms which were folded across the table top.

"Megan!" Mr. Jameson's voice startled her into raising her head to look at him.

"We are here for a reason, and it isn't to sleep!"

Megan made a face to Brittany and Ashley, but sat up straighter in her chair.

"Today I want to discuss with you the importance of education. I figured that would be appropriate as we move into a new school year."

"We've been in school three weeks already!"

Mr. Jameson looked at the student who had spoken. "A new

Bahá'í school year. Is that more correct, Jim?"

Jim didn't answer, but sank a little deeper into his chair.

Mr. Jameson turned back to the class. "So is education important?"

At first no one answered, then Brittany raised her hand. "Of course!"

"How do we know?...Megan?"

Megan shot a glance at Ashley.

"Because the Bahá'í writings tell us that it is," she answered as she yawned.

"Where?"

"What?"

"Where in the Bahá'í writings does it tell us that education is important?" replied Mr. Jameson.

The members of the class looked at each other, but no answer was volunteered until Brittany raised her hand and offered, "Abdu'l-Bahá said it."

"Very good, Brittany, but I want a more specific answer."

Mr. Jameson smiled as he said it, and somehow the whole class knew that they were in for something different. In the past, teachers had mostly talked to them or had them read aloud out of books.

They watched as he wheeled in a book cart laden with Bahá'í books.

"You each have approximately twenty minutes to find three quotes as to why education is important."

Random responses included:

"I don't know where to look!"

"You gotta be kidding!"

"There's too many books to look through!"

One clever student even asked, "Does anyone have the compilation on Bahá'í education?"

"Ah, good thought," replied Mr. Jameson, "but I have it safely hidden away."

The student groaned, and Mr. Jameson continued, "You are all in high school. It's time you got more active about learning the Faith. To get us started, I've got a few topics picked out, but then I want you to start coming up with ideas about what you want to learn."

"Can we work in groups?" asked Ashley. Research was not her strong point.

"Sure! Why don't you work with the people at your table?"

"No fair," called out Jim. "You guys have Brittany at your table."

Brittany beamed with pride as she answered, "Oh well! I gotta be with somebody!"

The three quotes Brittany, Ashley, and Megan found were:

"Arts, crafts and sciences uplift the world of being, and are conducive to its exaltation. Knowledge is as wings to man's life, and a ladder for his ascent."
—*Epistle to the Son of the Wolf*, p. 26

"Observe carefully how education and the arts of civilization bring honour, prosperity, independence and freedom to a government and its people."
—*The Secret of Divine Civilization*, p. 111

"Bahá'u'lláh has announced that inasmuch as ignorance and lack of education are barriers of separation among mankind, all must receive training and instruction."
—*The Promulgation of Universal Peace*, p. 300

The class discussed why education was important, but there was no one against it, so there wasn't much spark to add enthusiasm to the discussion. Education was mandatory in the U.S., so it wasn't a surprise at all that the Faith would count it so. The only time they had a good laugh was when Jim found the quote where Abdu'l-Bahá said that children should not be taught with books. He said he was going to show that to his social studies teacher. But no one really took the quote seriously. What would school be without books? All education centered around books. Abdu'l-Bahá must have been thinking about the time before books were so readily available to everyone.

"Do you really think Abdu'l-Bahá could have been wrong?" asked Mr. Jameson.

"Not really wrong," answered Brittany, "just speaking about a different time."

"But this is the Revelation for this time."

"Of course it is, but not every word written was about this time. This was written before the time of e-mail, for heaven's sake."

"I'll reply to that after I've found the right quote," said Mr. Jameson, smiling.

Even so, Brittany ended the session glowing with achievement as much as Ashley felt overwhelmed. Megan had mostly just tried to stay awake.

"Cheer up, Ashley, you did well. You found the quote from *The Promulgation of Universal Peace*. What's wrong with that?" asked Brittany.

"Nothing's wrong with it. But I felt like the part where it said "ignorance and lack of education are barriers of separation among mankind" was speaking directly to me."

"Oh, for heaven's sake, why?" put in Megan. "You're not

ignorant!"

"Well, I'm sure not smart!"

"Look," Megan said, "being smart doesn't make you a better person." She looked pointedly at Brittany, but Brittany ignored her.

"Besides," added Brittany, "ignorance really means uneducated. You're educated, so you're not ignorant. You're just—"

She paused, trying to find a word that wouldn't hurt Ashley's feelings.

"Nice work, Britt," said Megan, knowing full well that Brittany hated being called Britt.

"Yeah. Thanks a lot. I gotta go. Mom and Dad are waiting."

Megan elbowed Brittany as Ashley walked over toward her parents.

"Way to go, Brain! What were you thinking?"

"I was just trying to convince her that she wasn't ignorant!" defended Brittany.

"I don't think you managed it. There's my mom and dad. See you tomorrow."

Brittany looked around for her own mother. It wasn't difficult to find her. Look for the most beautiful woman at the gathering, and it would be her mother, Vanessa. She always looked like she just stepped out of a magazine, and Brittany felt huge whenever they walked side by side.

Vanessa owned her own realty business and had several agents working for her. With the present boom the economy was experiencing, money was coming in faster than it had even in the past, and they had always done well. Six years ago, Vanessa and her husband had gotten divorced, and she had felt a sense of pride when, during the settlement, she had been able to say that she had no need of alimony, thank you very much.

She had said she wanted no monthly checks reminding her of the...person she had been married to. Unfortunately, her attitude made it difficult for Brittany to enjoy the little time with her father that they had.

"What is it, Brittany? You look like you lost your best friend!" cooed Vanessa.

"Well, if I didn't, I deserve to."

"What happened?"

"I really don't want to talk about it, Mom."

"Okay...How 'bout going out for a nice lunch?"

Inwardly, Brittany cringed, but she only said, "Sure."

Vanessa really felt uncomfortable talking to Brittany about anything personal, and, unfortunately for Brittany, her mom always preferred to try to cheer her up with food. Brittany thought of it as the "don't cry, have a cookie" syndrome. She sometimes suspected that it was a way to keep her big to show off her mother's beauty by comparison. Of course, that wasn't fair. But let's face it, thought Brittany, life isn't fair.

Chapter Three

On Tuesday morning, Megan found Ashley right when Ashley was getting off the bus.

"What are you doing here so early?" asked Ashley.

One reason Megan's mom drove her to school is that Megan couldn't quite get ready in time for the bus. It was far more normal for her to come flying into class just as the bell was ringing.

"I just had to tell you what happened at play rehearsal yesterday!"

"Didn't you do a read through like usual at the first rehearsal?"

"Yeah, but guess what?! I get to kiss Kevin Bradley in the second act!"

Ashley frowned.

"What's the matter, Ashley? Jealous?"

"Oh, yeah, right. Like I'm Kevin's type. It just doesn't feel right, that's all."

"What do you mean?"

"I don't think we're supposed to be doing that sort of stuff."

"You gotta be kidding!"

"Remember what we studied in *The Advent of Divine Justice* last year? We're not really supposed to date, let alone go around kissing people."

"It's a play, Ashley! It's just pretend!"

Ashley could sense Megan's rising frustration, so decided to let it go.

"I think every other girl in school is going to wish she could be the one pretending with Kevin."

That was exactly the reaction that Megan had wanted in the first place, and she graced Ashley with a dazzling smile.

"I think so, too! Well, I'd better get to my locker, or I'll be late for English."

"See ya later!" called out Ashley, but she had a sort of weird feeling in her stomach. Something was wrong, and she wasn't sure what she could do about it.

When the feeling was still haunting her on Thursday, Ashley asked Megan if she could come and watch play rehearsal.

"Well," answered Megan, "Ms. Hillman doesn't like people coming in for no reason. It spoils the effect of the end product. You wanna paint some scenery or something?"

"Sure, as long as I don't have to draw it."

"Oh, no, you won't have to draw. We have kids from the art department come to do that."

Ashley sighed as her thoughts drifted along another path. She didn't belong to the art department or the drama department, or any other department. She didn't fit in anywhere.

"Ashley? Where did you go?" Megan said, laughing at her thoughtful friend.

Ashley snapped back to the present.

"Oh, sorry. I guess I'm spacey today. I'll be there after school, okay?"

"Okay, but how will you get home?"

"Mom said she'd pick me up at five. She's pretty good about that when I need her to be."

Megan just smiled and nodded. How a mom could be pretty good about something when she wouldn't do it every day was really beyond her.

Play rehearsal took place in the auditorium, and there was a large storage area adjacent to the stage where the scenery could be painted. Ashley tried to keep an ear open to hear what was going on in the actual rehearsal, but it was difficult. She didn't want to lose concentration and make a mistake. All she had to do was paint inside the lines of what the artists told her, so it wasn't too difficult, IF she kept her mind on her work.

Greg, one of the artists, came over to where Ashley was working.

"Wow! You're really working fast! This is great!"

Ashley blushed beet red as she muttered, "Thanks."

"You're working too fast for me. Why don't you take a little break while I get this next section drawn in?"

"Really?"

"Sure! Why not? Hard work should be rewarded." He looked right at Ashley and smiled.

She would probably have been more comfortable if she had recognized the familiar disappointment when someone looked at her face, but she saw none of it. Greg seemed to be looking right at her and not noticing how far from pretty she was. A butterfly seemed to flutter in her stomach, and she jumped.

"What's the matter?" Greg asked. "Are you all right, Ashley?"

"Just a chill, I guess. Maybe I need that break." She knew her face was even redder than it had been before, and she made a beeline to the sink to wash her hands before entering the auditorium. In an effort to keep from tripping over anything, she glued her eyes to the floor. There was stuff all over the place, and she was not famous for her grace. What made it worse was that she could feel Greg's eyes watching her as she walked away.

"He's probably thinking what a goof ball I am," she thought to herself.

As soon as she rounded the corner and knew she was out of his sight, she leaned against the wall as if to catch her breath. Greg was a senior, and she was only a sophomore. That she should know him was not surprising. He had even been nominated for Homecoming King this fall, being the star of the basketball team and all. Since their football team seldom had a winning season, the basketball players drew far more attention. But that Greg should know Ashley's name was beyond her comprehension.

"Weird. Definitely weird," she thought.

Her hands would not come completely clean, but once her coloring and breathing were somewhat back to normal, she headed out to watch the rehearsal.

Megan was doing a wonderful job. In Ashley's estimation, Megan was a much better at acting than Kevin Bradley was, but she admitted that she might be a little biased. Megan just looked so natural up there on the stage! And when she looked up at Kevin, she really did look like she was in love with him.

They were rehearsing the second act, and when the part for the kiss came up, Ms. Hillman said they could leave it out until later.

Kevin, however, had other ideas.

He said, "I always say, 'no time like the present.'" And he grabbed Megan before she even realized what was happening, and kissed her.

The same sick feeling that had been in Ashley's stomach on Tuesday morning came back again, confirming her fear that Megan was headed for trouble.

Megan was dumbfounded for an instant, then composed herself and managed a smile.

"That was perfect!" exclaimed Ms. Hillman. "Well done! Very convincing!"

"Want to see it again?" asked Kevin.

Ms. Hillman winked at him, but answered, "I don't think that will be necessary right now. I want to finish the scene before we stop for the day."

They went back to rehearsing, but Ashley felt as awful as Megan felt wonderful. Megan had been kissed by the cutest boy in school, even when the teacher had said that it wasn't necessary. She would construe that into believing that he had done it strictly because he wanted to. The idea made Ashley almost ill. She couldn't help remembering something in the Bahá'í writings from last year. What was it? She'd have to look it up when she got home.

September 22
Dear Diary,
I'm really worried about Megan. She's enjoying that attention Kevin's giving her too much. I know that sounds silly. How can you enjoy something too much? But something about it scares me.

I looked up one of the quotes I was thinking of when I got home today. Shoghi Effendi says in The Advent of Divine Justice *that "Such a chaste and holy life, with its implications of modesty, purity, temperance, decency, and clean-mindedness, involves no less than the exercise of moderation in all that pertains to dress, language, amusements, and all artistic and literary avocation." That's on page 25, in case I need to find it again.*

Maybe I'm scared because I don't think that Kevin's a real good example of clean-mindedness. Of that I'm pretty certain, according to his reputation. Of course, reputations are usually based on gossip, which is strictly forbidden in the Faith. Gosh! What's the best thing for me to do? Maybe I should just forget about it like Megan says. It's just that...

Megan knows what Kevin's reputation is, but she still seems attracted to him. Maybe that's what scares me...

By the way, Greg Morrison knew my name today when we were painting scenery together. Well, not really together, he drew, and I filled in between the lines. The only thing I can figure is that I must be famous for being the ugliest girl in school. The weirdest part is that he didn't make me feel ugly...he almost made me feel...

Don't be ridiculous...I'm just stupid.
—Ashley

Chapter Four

Because Ashley's mom often had to work late at the grocery store if there were a rush, she couldn't guarantee Ashley a ride home every day to enable Ashley to stay after school to work on sets. The nice thing about Mary Ann, Ashley's mom, was that she never just said "no" if something were inconvenient. She worked out with her boss that she could get off by 4:30 on Tuesdays and Thursdays no matter what so Ashley could stay late on those days.

Greg often managed to have Ashley work with him on the days that she was there. After all, he was a senior and in charge of sets, and if he said, "Ashley, you'll work with me today," she said, "Okay." He often commented on her hard work, and she was almost getting to the point where it didn't make her turn bright crimson when she heard him say it.

One particular Thursday, the phone in Ms. Hillman's office rang shortly before five o'clock. Not every teacher had a phone in their office, but Ms. Hillman had lobbied for one because she so frequently had students working late at night. They had to be able to reach their parents. Of course, Ms. Hillman considered it a moral victory for the arts because the coaches had phones in their offices, and she wasn't about to let the arts be second best, no matter how many other people thought that sports were the most important thing in school.

Ms. Hillman was out in the auditorium, so Greg answered the phone. "Yes, she's here. Just a minute."

He covered the receiver with his hand and called out, "Ashley, it's for you."

Immediately, Ashley knew something must be wrong. Her father was at work, and her mother should be on her way to pick Ashley up. Her little sister, Michelle, stayed at the neighbor's house until someone picked her up each day, so there was no one who should be calling her unless something was wrong.

When she got to the phone, her voice cracked with worry as she said, "Yes? This is Ashley O'Connor. What is it?"

"Gosh! Relax, Honey! It's just me. Your mom."

"What's wrong?"

"Nothing that bad. It's just that the car won't start. Mr. Miller, who works in the store, has been trying to see if he could get it to go, but it just won't budge. I'm having it towed to the repair shop, and I'll just have to wait there until your dad can pick me up after he gets off. Do you think Megan could take you home?"

"Gosh, no, Mom. This is Thursday. Megan has ballet on Thursday nights. There's no way her mom would have time to run me all the way home first. I'll just have to wait here until you and Dad can pick me up."

"I can take you home."

Ashley whirled to see Greg leaning against the doorway of Ms. Hillman's office. "Don't be silly!" said Ashley.

"Who's being silly?" asked her mom.

"Oh, it's nothing, Mom. Somebody here just offered to take me home."

"Oh, how nice! Who is it?"

"It's nobody you know, Mom."

"Oh, that's too bad. I don't want you riding with anyone I don't know."

Greg walked over to the desk where the phone and Ashley were.

"I'm serious. I'll take you home," he offered again.

"Thanks, but my mom doesn't let me ride with people she doesn't know."

He took the phone right out of her hand while he said, "Let me talk to her." Ashley's protest did no good.

"Mrs. O'Connor? This is Greg Morrison. Are you having car trouble?"

Silently, Ashley watched in horror and listened, desperately trying to imagine what her mother was saying to this boy on the phone.

"Where are you? That's only a few miles from here. Would you like me to pick you up, too? That way you could meet me."

Ashley was too much in shock to react. She just stared at Greg in disbelief.

"Oh, sure. I know where that is…No, it wouldn't be any trouble at all. Aren't we supposed to help people in need?…Okay, then, we'll leave here in a few minutes after we've washed out the paint brushes. Okay…Okay, I will. See you soon!"

He hung up the phone, and Ashley's contact with her mother was cut off. She didn't move. She didn't speak. She stood looking at Greg.

Finally, he said, "You wanna help me wash out these

brushes so we can go?"

She managed to squeak out, "Why are you doing this?"

"Why not? It's no big deal."

"Why should you go out of your way for me?"

"It's not that far out of my way, and I'd do it for anyone who thought they were going to be stuck here until who knew when, especially a girl.

"And wipe that knowing look off your face," he continued. "It's not being chauvinistic at all. You've gotta admit that more women get raped than men."

"I'm sorry. You're right. It's just not anything I ever felt in danger of."

"Now that's dangerous thinking."

"No. Just realistic."

"Not realistic. Stupid." And with that he turned to gather up the brushes and take them to the sink.

Neither one of them said anything more until the mess was cleaned up, and they were on their way out to Greg's car.

"I don't get you," Greg said.

"What do you mean?"

"One minute it sounds like you're assuming I must have ulterior motives to offer to take you home, and the next you're saying you think you're too plain-looking to get raped. Do you think I'm lower than the average rapist, or what?"

"What?!"

"You heard me." He got in and buckled his seat belt.

After Ashley had done the same, she swallowed hard and ventured, "I don't think you're lower than the average rapist." Her voice was scarcely more than a whisper, but she could tell that he heard her, and she was relieved that she wouldn't have to repeat it.

"Good. So what's your problem with me taking you home?"

"Look. You're a senior,-"

"Does that mean I can't be nice to a sophomore?"

"No! Of course not! I guess I just don't-"

"Don't what?"

"I guess I just don't understand why you'd want to."

"If the situation were reversed, if I were the sophomore and didn't have a way home, wouldn't you offer me a ride?"

"Of course, but—"

"But a guy isn't supposed to be thoughtful?"

Something came over her, and she didn't seem capable of stopping herself. "Look, why don't you stop interrupting me and listen!? I'm sorry if I bought into a stereotype, okay? I try not to be prejudiced, but I never realized that stereotyping jocks—"

He made a face.

"Sorry. Athletes was a kind of prejudice to have. Let's get serious here. You are probably going to be Homecoming King. You are the star forward of the basketball team. You are probably one of the most popular guys in the senior class. I, on the other hand, am so…plain, as you call it, that most of the kids in school don't know that I exist. My grades aren't good, I'm not an artist, I can't sing. Doesn't it seem a bit odd to you that you would even notice me, let alone offer to take me home? I mean, I'm not stupid enough to think that you're interested in me or anything, but for the life of me, I can't figure out why you would offer to take me home. Why be bothered? No one is gonna be impressed by it. It just doesn't make sense!"

All of a sudden, the torrent of words ran out of energy and came to a halt.

"Oh my gosh! I've never talked so much in my life!"

Greg pulled the car to the side of the road, put it in park, and turned towards Ashley.

"Look," he said, "being the 'star forward,' as you put it, doesn't make me any less of a human being than being 'plain' does for you."

Her eyes were hypnotized by his, and her voice was played out.

"To be perfectly honest, I noticed you last year, when you refused to wear your dresses short like the other girls. I met Megan last year in a play, and I know she's got a bad temper, but I've seen you calm her down when she was ranting and raving about something stupid.

"And when most kids come in to paint scenery, they do it to have a place to gossip after school. You never gossip…at rehearsals anyway, which I appreciate, but you also work hard, which I appreciate even more. I take my scenery very seriously, and it drives me nuts to see those other kids laughing and not being careful about where they put the paint.

"So, can we start over and just give each other credit for being human, and go from there?"

No words would come out of her mouth. She had to answer by nodding her head in ascent.

"And by the way," he added, "I am interested in you."

He smiled at her as he started the car, but not even the roar of the engine could shake Ashley out of her dream.

It had to be a dream, didn't it? She pinched herself on her leg, and it hurt. Maybe it wasn't a dream.

Chapter Five

As Brittany and Ashley walked into their Bahá'í school class, Mr. Jameson greeted them saying, "Good morning, ladies. Oh, Brittany! I keep forgetting to give you that quote I was telling you about before."

"What quote is that?" asked Brittany, frowning.

"Remember on the first day of classes when we found a passage where Abdu'l-Bahá talked about students not learning from books?" he asked. "You said that he wasn't wrong, but he was speaking about a different time. I believe you said something like, 'This was written before the time of e-mail, for heaven's sake,' didn't you?"

"Yeah, I guess so."

"Well, I want you to read this quote for me, please. It's not from Abdu'l-Bahá, like I thought it was, but it is Shoghi Effendi from the year 1938."

He handed *The World Order of Bahá'u'lláh* to Brittany. She read from page 203 where he indicated.

"A mechanism of world inter-communication will be devised, embracing the whole planet, freed from national hindrances and restrictions, and functioning with marvelous swiftness and perfect regularity."

"Wow! That's incredible!" exclaimed Ashley.

"What's incredible?" asked Megan, who was just coming in.

"Shoghi Effendi knew there was going to be e-mail back in 1938!"

"What?"

Brittany explained, "This is a quote Mr. Jameson showed me this morning. Shoghi Effendi didn't really call it 'e-mail,' but he referred to a system of communication that would be instantaneous between East and West."

"Cool!" replied Megan.

By this time, the rest of the class had trickled in and were ready to go.

"We've been looking through the Writings for a few weeks now," began Mr. Jameson. "Can anyone explain to the rest of the class why we've been doing it?"

Someone volunteered, "Because education is important?"

"Well, that's true. What else?"

Twenty pairs of eyes darted around the room, some to meet friends, some to inspect the ceiling, and others to be suddenly concerned with a wrinkle found in a pair of jeans.

"Okay," said Mr. Jameson, "let's try this. How are most of your classes in school conducted? What is the teacher's role?"

"The teacher mostly stands up in front and explains things." Brittany took over. "Students take notes—"

"—or not!" threw in Jim for a laugh.

Ignoring him, Brittany continued, "—and try to remember everything the teacher says so they can do well on the test."

"Which one of the Faith's principles ties into what we're discussing?" asked Mr. Jameson.

No response.

Suddenly, Ashley had an idea. It was almost as if lightening had struck her, and she blurted out the answer before she had time to stop herself. Usually, she was like most students who struggled in a classroom setting, choosing to be as nondescript as possible and never volunteering information in fear of being wrong. But today, as soon as the idea was in her head, it came out of her mouth.

"Independent investigation!"

Many of the members of the class turned to stare at Ashley in amazement. She felt her cheeks get hot and knew they were an annoying shade of red.

"Exactly the answer I was looking for, Ashley! Good job! Now can you explain why our discussion pertains to independent investigation, or would you like someone else to do it?"

"I'll do it," offered Brittany. Ashley often leaned on Brittany to explain things for her. It saved Ashley from embarrassment, and gave Brittany another chance to shine. But this time, Ashley tried it herself.

"Thanks, Brittany, but I think I can at least get started.

"Religion is a personal thing. If we only come to Bahá'í school because our parents make us, it's their religion, not ours. The only way we can make it ours is if we ask the questions, and we find the answers in the Writings. I think that's why Bahá'u'lláh said that everyone should do their own investigating."

Usually when a hush came over the class, it was because too many of them had been up too late the night before, but this time, they were staring at Ashley in appreciation.

Mr. Jameson was quick to point out. "Great observation, Ashley! Of course, none of us can interpret the Writings for anyone else, but I think you've really gotten at the heart of why I wanted all of you to do some research.

"You are all in high school. Soon you'll be going off to live your own lives, whether that's to college, trade school, a job, or getting married."

That last comment got a few chuckles, but Mr. Jameson continued, "This is the time for you to figure out if being a Bahá'í is going to be a part of that life."

After class, Megan, Brittany, and Ashley walked out together as usual, but they were quiet, which was definitely not usual.

Vanessa, Brittany's mom, walked towards them saying, "We have to leave right away, Brittany. One of my agents is sick, and I have to do her open house this afternoon."

As she noticed that all three of the girls were continuing to walk in silence, she asked, "What's the matter?"

Brittany recovered first.

"Nothing's the matter, Mom," she replied. "Mr. Jameson just reminded us that we're growing up."

"Well, of course you're growing up, Sweetie!"

"I know, Mom. Never mind. I'll see you two tomorrow in school!"

"Bye, Brittany!"

Vanessa had had to do many an open house on a Sunday afternoon, so Brittany was used to it. But this Sunday was particularly beautiful, and for some reason Brittany did not understand herself, her mother's pending absence irritated her. If she had known ahead of time, she could have made some plans with someone.

Who was she kidding? She never did anything with anyone

outside of school. Her mom's schedule really limited when and where she could drive Brittany, and there weren't really any kids her age, at least that she cared to spend any time with, who lived close enough to walk or ride bikes.

"Life will sure be different when I get my license!" she thought to herself.

Yeah, right. As if getting her license would suddenly make people want to spend time with her. Who was she kidding? Ashley and Megan were probably the only two people who tolerated her, and they were both busy with play rehearsals right now. Other kids didn't like her because she was fat. That was it. Of course, there were other kids who were fat, even bigger than her, that seemed to have plenty of friends.

They were jealous because she was so smart. But that wasn't fair! What did they expect her to do? Hide the fact that she understood things just to make them more comfortable? It wasn't her fault! Brittany hated days like today.

"You're awfully quiet today, Honey. Is everything okay?" asked Vanessa.

"Fine, Mom. Everything's peachy."

"Are you angry at me for something?"

"I wish you had told me you had to work this afternoon. I don't feel like being alone."

"Sarah only paged me half an hour ago. She woke up today with the flu."

"I'll bet she did."

"For your information, Brittany Myers, Sarah is pregnant, and has a perfect right to be sick. Someday you'll understand."

Brittany hated it when her mother took that "you don't know everything, young lady" attitude. She knew that she was in a bad mood, though, so decided saying nothing would be better than saying something that might get her into more trouble.

Vanessa misunderstood her silence, however, and continued, "I was going to offer to have you put on a nice dress and come with me, but I don't think that would be a good idea."

Tears stung Brittany's eyes. Now even her mother didn't want to be with her. Great. But all she said was, "Whatever."

Chapter Six

Ashley was walking down the hall towards the bathroom. It always amazed her that the school could be so creepy when almost everyone had gone home. She knew that it wasn't even dark yet outside, but still shadows made her feel as if she were in a horror movie, and as if something or someone was going to jump out at her at any second. Almost without being aware of it, she began to walk faster.

As she turned a corner, she bumped into something. It made a funny noise and seemed to move in two different directions at once. Ashley screamed and felt a hand come over her mouth. It was trying to smother her!

"Oh, Ashley, it's you! You scared us to death!"

It was Megan.

And as Ashley calmed down, she realized that the hand over her mouth belonged to Kevin Bradley. Suddenly, a wave of understanding crashed over her, and she turned so red she was afraid they would see it even in the dark.

Kevin removed his hand.

"Are you done screaming?" he asked.

"Yes. I-I-I was just-" Ashley's discomfort was now more from finding Megan and Kevin together in the dark than it was from being frightened, and Megan figured it out.

"Hey, were you headed for the bathroom? I'll go with you," she offered lightly.

Ashley stammered. "No...that's okay. I don't want to disturb you."

"Don't be silly," replied Megan. "You're not disturbing us. You just scared us, that's all."

"Yeah," put in Kevin, "we were just...practicing. Yeah, practicing."

He smiled, looking amused, but Ashley knew that there was no good reason for his amusement. He either thought she was too dumb to understand, or he thought getting caught with Megan was funny. Ashley didn't appreciate either one.

"Yeah," Megan repeated. "Practicing."

Ashley headed on down the hall as quickly as she had been walking before. Megan came running after her.

"Hey! Slow down!"

Ashley kept walking. When she entered the bathroom, Megan came right on in after her.

"What do you want me to do, apologize?" Megan asked indignantly.

"For what? It's your life."

"And you think I'm ruining it?"

"It's none of my business."

"You're right there!"

Ashley just looked at her friend.

Megan suddenly looked worried. "You're not thinking of telling, are you?"

"Oh, thanks a lot. That's giving me a lot of credit!"

"I'm sorry. You're right. Then why are you looking at me like that?"

"I think you're making a big mistake, and I care about you 'cause you're my friend, okay?"

"What's the big mistake? You think my parents would be really upset if they knew? I'm not so sure. This is a new century, kiddo. I think they understand that, even if you don't."

One thing that got Ashley upset more than anything else was someone referring to her difficulty understanding things. She lost her temper.

"I think I understand life in the new century more than you do! A new century means that the Lesser Peace is at hand! It means that our job of teaching and being good examples is more important than ever!"

"You're not being fair! I go to Bahá'í school, and I work on a lot of teaching projects! I'm a good Bahá'í, but this is my private life!"

"What part of your life is private from God?!"

With that, Ashley left the room. She would have slammed the door for emphasis, but it was on one of those pressurized hinges that prevent it from ever being slammed. Kevin was still out in the hall waiting for Megan, but Ashley went past him without saying a word.

She hated arguments! What was she doing? Megan was one of her best friends. Tears began running down her cheeks making it hard to see in the poor light. When she opened the stage door, she expected to find the set area empty because everyone else had left before she had gone to the bathroom. Just her luck. Greg had forgotten something and come back just in time to see her burst through the door crying.

"Ashley! What is it?" he asked as he came immediately over

to her.

"Nothing."

"Oh, yeah. I can see that. Now what gives?"

"I just lost my temper at Megan. I can't believe I yelled at my friend!"

"Did she deserve it?"

"Who deserves having a friend yell at them?" she asked, and the tears started anew. Greg put his arm around her and offered her his handkerchief. Without thinking about it, Ashley leaned her head against his shoulder as she cried.

At that moment, Megan and Kevin came through the door. Megan's eyes were red, but her mood changed quickly from hurt to anger when she saw Ashley with Greg. "Well, well, well," she said with a wicked tone in her voice. "What have we here?"

"She's upset," answered Greg softly.

Ashley turned towards Megan, not yet comprehending what Megan was implying. As the realization broke through, she flushed.

"Maybe you two should talk this out when you're both a little calmer," suggested Greg.

"What did she do? Tell you everything?" Megan was aghast.

"All she told me was that you two had had an argument," defended Greg.

"I'll bet. Come on, Kevin. How 'bout you walk me out to the parking lot? Let's leave these two alone."

Ashley finally found her voice. "We don't need to be alone, Megan!"

"Really, Megan," added Kevin, "think about what you're saying."

The condescension in his tone was like a knife in Ashley's heart. It was all too obvious that he thought Ashley too ugly to attract someone like Greg.

"Just get out of here!" Greg yelled, and he put his arm back around Ashley's shoulder in a protective gesture.

When they had gone, Greg lifted Ashley's face with his free hand.

"By next week, you'll probably be best friends again. Don't worry too much. Megan's got a bad temper. And people always say hurtful things when they're upset. It's part of what keeps humans from finding too much happiness."

"Thanks, but you don't understand. Not saying hurtful things is something I've always tried very hard to do. And now I've said terrible things, and to one of my best friends. I feel awful."

"I know. I've felt that way myself. We just have to apologize and try to do better the next time."

"Yeah, right." Ashley was almost as upset about her blowing up and not being a good example to Greg, Kevin, and Megan as she was about the things she had actually said.

"Come on. I'll walk you outside," offered Greg.

"Thanks. You're a good friend." And as her own words reminded her of what a good friend she had not been, the tears burned in her eyes again.

Chapter Seven

When Megan came into Bahá'í school that week, she made a point of sitting at a different table than Ashley and Brittany. She was a popular girl at high school, so there were always kids who were willing, even eager to have her sit by them.

Mr. Jameson, however, was not insensitive to his students, and when someone suddenly sat with different people than usual, a red flag went up for him.

"Anyone have something special they want to discuss today?" he asked.

No one said a word.

"Okay. Where does world peace begin?"

"I don't get what you're asking," said Jim.

"Let me try it this way. What would you say is the fundamental principle underlying the Faith?"

Brittany felt confident about that one. "To recognize God and worship Him. You know what it says in the daily obligatory prayer: 'Thou hast created me to know Thee and to worship

Thee. '"

"I think you may have hit on the very purpose of creation, Brittany, but let's build on that." He scanned through the ever-present book shelves to find the exact book he was looking for. "Ah! Here it is!" he exclaimed in triumph. "In Bahá'í Marriage and Family Life on page 28, it quotes Bahá'u'lláh saying: 'After man's recognition of God, and becoming steadfast in His Cause the station of affection, of harmony, of concord and of unity is superior to that of most other goodly deeds...'

"So what is superior to most other goodly deeds?" he asked.

One person called out, "Affection!"

"Good listening!" replied Mr. Jameson. "What else?"

A few more people got brave enough to answer.

"Unity!'

"Great! What else?"

"Harmony!"

"And the last one?"

No one could remember.

"That's okay," said Mr. Jameson. "You did well. The last one was concord, which essentially means the same thing as the other words.

"Let me read one more quote that catches my eye on that same page: 'At all times hath union and association been well-pleasing in the sight of God, and separation and dissension abhorred'."

"Okay," said Zivar, "we understand that we're supposed to get along. That's no surprise. Where are you going with this?"

"Let me read one more quote and see if you can figure out where I'm going. On page 32, it says: 'If we Bahá'í s cannot attain to cordial unity among ourselves, then we fail to realize the main purpose for which the Báb, Bahá'u'lláh, and the

Beloved Master lived and suffered'."

When no one volunteered any guess, Megan couldn't stand the silence anymore.

"The direction he's going is to say that I must not understand the main purpose of being a Bahá'í if I can't be nice to everyone, including Ashley, whom he noticed I did not sit by today for the first time. Am I right, Mr. Jameson?"

"Partially. I would never imply that you didn't understand what it was to be a Bahá'í. No one can or has the right to try to answer that question except you. The words are Shoghi Effendi's, by the way.

"I'd just like to say that nothing we can do in here would be more important than helping ourselves learn how to stay unified even when we disagree, which is healthy."

Brittany was horrified. "Do you want the class to consult about Ashley and Megan's fight?! It's too private!"

"Actually, it was a Bahá'í issue that we fought about, wasn't it Ashley?" Megan's voice could have a painful edge to it when she chose it to, and it certainly did this time.

"I guess so."

Members of the class were torn between being able to know what had gone on and being terrified that one of their own arguments might be offered up for class discussion. Surprisingly enough, it was Jim who offered insight.

"Look, on one hand, the Writings say to consult in all things. On the other, it's clear that we're not supposed to do anything like confessing sins. So I'd say that it's totally up to Ashley and Megan if they want us to talk about what went on. Everybody in here could feel the ice between them this morning. If they want to sacrifice their privacy to give us a chance to help and to learn to consult better, that's great. But if they'd rather work it out themselves, I can certainly understand that."

"I completely agree with Jim," said Mr. Jameson.

"Kinda scary, isn't it?" put in Zivar, and everyone laughed.

For a few moments, nothing was said, but then Megan looked at Ashley.

"What do you think?" she asked.

"I don't care. Whatever you want…"

"Okay."

"Let's do it like a debate!" said Brittany. "I'm on the debate team, so I can help. First we'll let Ashley tell her side, and then Megan will get a chance for rebuttal—"

"For what?" asked Jim.

"For rebuttal. That's when—"

"I'm terribly sorry to interrupt you, Brittany, but rather than learn the ins and outs of debate which is not really part of the Faith, why don't we try to use the process of consultation?"

Teachers usually praised Brittany for her good ideas. She not only was taken aback, but she felt chastised as well. Not another word would pass her lips for the rest of the discussion that day.

Mr. Jameson had a feeling that he needed to apologize to Brittany or at least soothe her hurt feelings, but that could launch into an entirely different topic, and he wanted to go with Megan and Ashley right now.

"Brittany, will you please stay after class for a few minutes today?"

Several students could not resist the "brain" having to stay after. There were many oo's and ah's, along with comments like:

"Oooo! You're in trouble now!"

"You'll probably have to see the principal!"

"That's enough!" called Mr. Jameson. "She's not in trouble at all! Let's put our energies in a more positive direction, shall we?"

Megan began. "I know the Writings say that we're supposed to be chaste and stuff, but Ashley thinks that my being in the play doesn't come up to those standards because I kiss my leading man and wear tight pants with a blouse that comes off my shoulders. I think she's being extreme and has no right to say anything anyway."

To Ashley, it sounded as if everyone in the class already believed Megan was right, but they expected to hear from her, so she had to say something.

"I do worry about Megan. But I didn't even say anything until she chased me into the bathroom and made me angry. I even said it was her life. When she asked me if I thought she was ruining it, I said it was none of my business, and she told me I was right."

The class turned back towards Megan.

"Is that true?" asked Jim.

Megan's voice was small as she whispered, "Yes." But she gathered strength enough to add, "But even when somebody says it's none of their business, you can tell what they're thinking. And I could tell that Ashley thought I was doing something really wrong."

"Wait a minute," said Zivar. "I don't get this. You were rehearsing the play and Ashley interrupted to tell you she thought you were being inappropriate, and you chased her into the bathroom?"

This time it was Megan's turn to flush red.

"No, no. It was at the end of rehearsal. We...bumped into each other in the hall. Isn't that right, Ashley?"

"Yeah. I bumped right into th—...her."

"I still don't get it," said Zivar.

"I might," put in Jim. "Let me ask one question. Megan,

43

were you alone in the hallway when Ashley bumped into you?" Megan's face went white. It was Ashley who found words to speak.

"Of course she was alone! She was coming back from the bathroom, and I was going towards it. I came around the corner and plowed into her. We were both scared half out of our wits."

"Well," Mr. Jameson put in hurriedly, "I think we probably have enough details! It seems to me the real issue here is at what point does behaving like a normal teenager in our society become not being chaste by the Bahá'í definition. Right?"

Megan betrayed her discomfort by speaking too fast. "Yes, that's definitely it, Mr. Jameson. You hit the nail right on the head. I'm just being normal, not unchaste."

"Okay, class. Find some quotes to shed light on this spiritual issue."

From *Lights of Guidance*, p.98-100, the students found:

"Dancers may appear, but great care should be used that they are not indecently clad or the dances vulgar in any way."

"...There is also no harm in taking part in dramas. Likewise in cinema acting. The harmful thing, nowadays, is not the art itself, but the unfortunate corruption which often surrounds these arts. As Bahá'ís we need to avoid none of the arts, but acts and the atmosphere that sometimes go with these professions we should avoid."

"...Although on principle there is no objection if any believer wishes to become a cinema actor, yet in view of the excessive corruption that now prevails along such a line of occupation, the Guardian would not advise any believer to choose this kind of profession, unless he finds this to be the *only* means of earning his livelihood."

"Whatever is written should not transgress the bounds of

tact and wisdom, and in the words used, there should lie hid the property of milk, so that the children of the world may be nurtured therewith, and attain maturity. We have said in the past that one word hath the influence of spring and causeth hearts to become fresh and verdant, while another is like unto blight which causeth the blossoms and flowers to wither. . . "

And in *Bahá'í Marriage and Family Life*, p. 20-22:
"Purity and chastity have been, and still are, the most great ornaments for the handmaidens of God. . ."
"Say: He is not to be numbered with the people of Baha who followeth his mundane desires, or fixeth his heart on things of the earth…if he met the fairest and most comely of women, he would not feel his heart seduced by the least shadow of desire for her beauty. Such an one, indeed, is the creation of spotless chastity."
"Such a chaste and holy life, with its implications of modesty, purity, temperance, decency, and clean-mindedness, involves no less than the exercise of moderation in all that pertains to dress, language, amusements, and all artistic and literary avocations. It demands daily vigilance in the control of one's carnal desires and corrupt inclination. It calls for the abandonment of a frivolous conduct, with its excessive attachment to trivial and often misdirected pleasures. It requires total abstinence from all alcoholic drinks, from opium, and from similar habit-forming drugs. It condemns the prostitution of art and literature, the practices of nudism and of companionate marriage, infidelity in marital relationships, and all manner of promiscuity, of easy familiarity, and of sexual vices. It can tolerate no compromise with the theories, the standards, the habits, and the excesses of a decadent age. Nay rather it seeks to demonstrate, through the dynamic force of its

example, the pernicious character of such theories, the falsity of such standards, the hollowness of such claims, the perversity of such habits, and the sacrilegious character of such excesses."

"I don't even know what half this stuff means," said David.

"Me neither."

"I can tell you one thing," said Megan. "'It can tolerate no compromise' means that moderation in all things doesn't include moral behavior."

"You mean that Bahá'u'lláh really does expect us to not date and be freaks?"

Quietly, Ashley answered, "Not freaks, examples. Positive examples to help show people the way to God."

Each mind in the room was churning. They were all fully aware of how popular Megan was and Ashley was not. They knew how many kids made fun of Ashley for the clothes she wore, and for the first time they realized that they may have just been given a glimpse into why she did it. Did Bahá'u'lláh want them all to be as laughed at as Ashley? Did He really expect them to not have girlfriends or boyfriends?

The bell rang.

"I think we'd better continue this discussion next week, don't you?" asked Mr. Jameson.

They looked like zombies leaving the class, each one absorbed in his own thoughts.

Chapter Eight

"Cut! Cut!" called Ms. Hillman from the back of the auditorium where she had been watching the rehearsal. "Take five, everybody! Megan! Come here, please!"

No one said a word as they left the stage. Megan probably would have felt better if they had teased her. Normally in a situation like this, they would have given her a bad time. But she knew exactly why Ms. Hillman was calling for her, and so did everyone else.

"Okay, Megan, what's going on?"

Megan hung her head and muttered, "I don't know."

"If you don't know, nobody does. Now come on. What gives? Did you have an argument with Kevin?"

Eyes flashing, Megan defended herself. "Kevin and I have no relationship whatsoever! Whether I have an argument with him or not would not affect my acting!"

"Well, something sure is! And maybe if you had a relationship it would help."

"No way!" cried Megan. But as her situation seemed more and more desperate, she slumped into one of the cushioned seats. Was there any way she could get Ms. Hillman to understand? She didn't think she understood herself.

"Some kids…," she began.

"Yes?"

"Some kids think I've been acting like a " She couldn't say it.

"Hm-m-m-m-m. Like a 'hussy'?"

"I guess."

"Well, it's better than the word you were thinking of, and probably more accurate anyway."

Ms. Hillman slowly took off her glasses and rubbed the bridge of her nose with her left hand. Every one of her students knew that was the sign that she was considering something important, and they should remain quiet. She ran her fingers through her dyed red hair, cradling her head in her arm as if to support it through the great effort it was exerting.

Finally, she replaced her glasses and said, "Megan, you have a talent for the stage. Not many people, especially ones your age, have the gift of feeling comfortable in front of a crowd. Fewer still have the ability to truly become someone else for a brief period of time and draw the audience with them into the fantasy.

"Your character is sexy, confident, and, shall we say, available. That doesn't mean that you, Megan, are sexy or available. You are merely the actress playing the part. For these next two weeks, I want you to continue to act as if you are totally in love with Kevin. If other students believe that you are, then you can take that as a sign that you are doing a good job. After the show's over, then you can go back to being 'plain old Megan,' and I don't care if you ever speak to him again.

"Do you think you can do that?"

Megan took heart. "So if they think…those things about me, it means I'm doing a good job?"

"The best. Remember, you are an actress—not a, shall we say, 'hussy'."

Tension left Megan through a prolonged sigh.

"Thanks, Ms. Hillman. I feel better now."

"Thank goodness. Okay, everybody!" she yelled, "Let's get back to work." Ms. Hillman's voice could be heard everywhere in the auditorium and back stage. It was amazing.

Kevin walked straight over to Megan.

"So is everything okay?" he asked.

She flashed one of her gorgeous, friendly smiles. "Better than okay."

"All right! I was afraid you were mad at me, or something."

"No, I was mad at myself, I guess. It doesn't matter now."

He put his arm around her.

"That's nice to know. I was hoping we could go out Saturday night—maybe a movie and pizza. How does that sound?"

Megan swore there were butterflies doing cartwheels in her stomach as she gazed into Kevin's deep brown eyes.

"It sounds good to me," she smiled.

"All right!" Then his voice dropped so that she could barely hear him, and he leaned down towards her ear. "Maybe we could go over some of our scenes."

The next thing she knew, he kissed her ear, and her butterflies went so crazy that she had to shake herself to figure out what scene Ms. Hillman was instructing them to begin.

Backstage, Greg watched Ashley as she painted. Her mind was obviously somewhere else, and also judging from the quality of Megan's work so far on stage, he guessed that he knew where it was.

When no one was close enough to hear, he asked, "So you and Megan haven't worked things out yet?"

Ashley was startled out of her thoughts. Shaking her head slowly, she said, "No, she's still not speaking to me."

"She'll get over it. If I know Megan, her temper flares, but fizzles out before too long."

"How do you know her so well?"

He shrugged. "I work on all the plays except for the one they do each year that interferes with basketball. She had good parts in the musical and two of the contest entries last year."

"That was pretty unusual for a freshman, wasn't it?"

"Yeah, most freshmen and sophomores get small parts, but she's a natural." When Ashley frowned, he knew he had made things worse instead of better. "Why is that bad? You don't think I'm interested in her or anything, do you?"

She stared at him with wide eyes. The ideas he got from her facial expressions often had nothing to do with the thoughts she was having, and it often surprised her when his comments seemed to have nothing to do with the conversation.

Hesitatingly, she began, "I don't know if you're interested in her or not, but that has nothing to do with why I frowned."

Whether he was convinced or not, she wasn't sure. It was almost as if he were hurt at her indifference about his caring about someone else, which made no sense whatsoever. Anyway, all he said was, "So why don't you tell me why you were frowning."

"I don't know if I can explain it."

"Well, give it a shot, and I'll try to help you out."

She took a deep breath.

"Sunday in Bahá'í school we talked about how we should be examples to try to lead others back to God."

"You don't mean that you feel that as a society we've

strayed, do you?"

His expression was shock, and all she could do was stare at him. When he could hold it no longer, he burst out laughing.

"I was kidding!"

"Oh." Then quietly she added, "I thought you were making fun of me."

The laughter left his face.

"I would never do that," he said.

Ashley felt the warmth surging up to her face and knew that her skin would be infuriatingly red, so she looked quickly away. Why couldn't she look like she had a permanent tan like her father?

"Anyway," she continued. "Megan feels like I'm saying she's not being a good example."

"Because of what happened last week?"

"Yeah."

"Well, is she being a good example?"

"It's not my place to say!" she replied. "What Megan does is between her and God!"

"Now that's a unique attitude," he quipped. "Most kids have plenty to say about what others should be doing."

There was really no reply to make.

Greg continued, "At the same time, if you are worried about her, as you obviously are, it would be easy for her to interpret that as your thinking she's doing the wrong thing."

"Yes. Yes, it would," Ashley agreed. . "But in my heart, I don't think I can just act like I believe what she's doing is a good idea, even if it is none of my business. After all, the Writings are pretty clear about wearing sexy clothes and all that. But on the other hand, wouldn't it be wrong for her to stop acting? I mean, if she has a talent, God gave her that talent, and it would be bad if she ignored it, wouldn't it?"

"Whew! That's a tough one!"

"That's why I was frowning," she said.

"I guess that's nice to know. I mean, that it wasn't anything I said or anything. But I sure don't have any good advice to give."

"I'm glad you listened anyway. It's not exactly a thing I can talk to my mom about."

"Not hardly. But I wish I could help."

"So do I!" replied Ashley, laughing.

He laughed with her, but then added, "You know, until Megan works out what the right thing for her to do is, you're like her conscience lurking about the stage."

"Great," she replied. "That's just what I wanted to hear."

"Sorry. Maybe I shouldn't have said it."

"No, you were right. Just 'cause it's no fun to hear doesn't make it the wrong thing to say."

"Well, at least let me add that it's Megan who's having trouble with her conscience. You should go on being who you are."

"Who knows what that is?"

"You do."

"Maybe."

Suddenly, Greg stood up.

"Look at that! We got this whole panel done while we were talking! We'd better call it quits for today, though. I promised your mom I'd have you home before 5:30 on days that rehearsals didn't go into the evening."

Ashley turned her head to try to look like she was looking for the paint lid. Of course, she was blushing, and she was trying to hide it. Last week when he had walked her out to her mom's car after the encounter with Megan and Kevin, he had asked her mom if she could start staying after school every day. He made the situation look like they would never be able to finish before the performances next week if he didn't have her there every day, and then he graciously offered to drive Ashley home so it wouldn't inconvenience her mother. Much to her surprise, Mary Ann had said that it would be fine.

For basically the next two weeks, Ashley would be riding home when play practice got over with the senior who had been voted Homecoming King by the entire school. Life was weird.

When she got home, Ashley went up to her diary as soon as she could.

Dear Diary,

I don't know what I'm going to do about Megan. Of course, I don't know if there's anything I can do. She's always been nice to me for some reason I never understood. Maybe she's just waking up and realizing she doesn't need me for a friend.

If what Greg says is right, and I am like her conscience, then I don't blame her for not wanting to be around me. On the other hand, who wants to be someone else's conscience? That's sure to make me popular at school!

But it's nice to think that Greg doesn't mind my being so weird. Sometimes I even think he likes me being different, but that's impossible.

God, what do You want me to do? If we're supposed to look for the good in people, shouldn't I appreciate Megan's talent more? But I can't believe you want me to let her believe that wearing revealing clothes and "practicing" in the hall are things You want us to do!

What about being unified even if in the wrong? It's more important to be unified than to have the "right" answer...So I should stick by Megan no matter what?

What about "consorting not with the ungodly?" Do we

pretend that we believe what they're doing is right? Do we avoid them for fear that they will influence us?

Mom and Dad say that if the Writings seem to conflict with each other, the problem is in our understanding. Well, I'm willing to admit that the problem is with my understanding, but that doesn't help me know what to do!

****************ACK!!!! *************** HELP!

Good grief! I'm going to do my homework.

—Ashley

Chapter Nine

Ashley walked right over to Brittany at Bahá'í school and sat down.

"How are you?" she asked. "I feel like I haven't seen you all week!"

"That's because you haven't," replied Brittany with a chill in her voice.

"I've been working on sets for the play," Ashley explained. "You get busy sometimes, too, you know."

"Oh, I know, and I'm sorry. I don't know what's come over me lately. I feel like I've been in a bad mood all week."

"Did Mr. Jameson talk to you after class last Sunday?"

"Yeah. He apologized for embarrassing me in front of the class, but pointed out all over again that debate was probably not the best format for Bahá'í school."

"Are you okay with that?"

Brittany's answer was cut off by Mr. Jameson saying he was ready to start class, but Brittany couldn't help thinking that most other kids would not have bothered to ask if she were okay with something a teacher said. Ashley was really sensitive to her feelings. She wished she could be more like Ashley.

"Okay, everybody! Let's get going! Would someone volunteer to say a prayer?"

Zivar read a prayer about meetings.

"I guess this isn't really a meeting, but I thought we might need all the help we could get," she said.

"I quite agree," confirmed Mr. Jameson. "Jim, would you update those who weren't here last week about our discussion?"

Reluctantly, Jim complied. "Mostly, we started trying to figure out how normal we could be and still be Bahá'í s."

Mr. Jameson squinted his face into a doubtful 'I have to think if I can accept that one' expression.

"What?" asked Jim. "Isn't that what we talked about?"

A slow nod of agreement.

"Close, anyway," responded Mr. Jameson. "Anyone want to elaborate?"

"To what?"

"Elaborate. Take the idea further."

Brittany answered, "I'll try."

The whole class looked at her as if she said she were flying to Rio the next day.

Brittany never 'tried' anything from their point of view. She always knew the answers.

"Go ahead, Brittany," said Mr. Jameson.

"Well, from the Writings we found last week, it seems like we're expected not to be 'normal' teenagers, as Jim would say. We should dress conservatively, not use bad language, and probably not even date. So the question is: How can we follow the Writings and not be total geeks?"

If anyone in the room was considered a 'geek,' it was Brittany. The fact that she chose that word made everyone uncomfortable enough to not reply.

As if on cue, that was the moment in which Megan made her entrance. She looked utterly exhausted.

"What time did you finally get in last night, Megan?" Her words were like ice. "What business is it of yours, Jim?"

"Well," he quipped, "at least her tongue's awake."

Everyone laughed at that one, except Megan, of course, but Jim wasn't quite finished.

"Did you have a good time with Kevin last night?"

The class began to buzz with reaction.

"Just how did you happen to know that I was out with Kevin last night?"

Jim really had not set out to embarrass Megan, but he could think of no other way to make sure she knew she had been the topic of conversation in the football locker room Friday after practice. They weren't friends, other than being in the same Bahá'í school class. There was no way he could just waltz up to her and say, "I think you're making a big mistake here, kiddo." So he let her know the only way he knew how, and that was through teasing.

"I guess he talked to Jose about it, and Jose was talking to all of us after football practice Friday about how lucky Kevin was. It seems a lot of guys think you're…" he paused for just a moment, "good lookin.'"

Megan was horrified, as Jim had known she would be at being a topic in a locker room, but her only reply was, "Gee. Thanks for the compliment, Jim."

As the buzzing intensified, Mr. Jameson jumped in to control the class.

"Okay, okay. Settle down. I think there are more aspects of

the problems of living a Bahá'í life than we touched on last week, but Jim and Brittany have given us plenty to get started with. Let's start with clothes. That might be the easiest."

"Fine," said Anita, eager to help relieve the tension if she could. "It's one of my favorite subjects. I think I ought to be able to wear anything I want without having my mom yell at me."

"Hm-m-m. Why does she yell?"

With a high pitched voice thick with sarcasm, Anita answered, "My skirts are too short. My shirt is too long. I look sloppy. Or my shirt is too short and shows my stomach. Big deal."

"Why does she care? No, wait. Let's keep parents out of this for now. Why did Shoghi Effendi say we should dress conservatively?"

Blank faces.

"You see," said Mr. Jameson. "I know I'm not in your shoes, but I see this as an issue between you guys and God, not between you and your parents really."

"But it changes it when you put it that way," protested Jim.

"Am I being unfair?"

No one in the class including Jim could make a case that Mr. Jameson was being unfair.

"Okay. Why do the Writings tell us to dress conservatively?"

Ashley timidly raised her hand.

"Ashley?"

"To be dignified?"

"Ooo…I like that answer! Why do we need to be dignified?"

"Because we're God's children?"

"Sure! Anybody else?"

"'Noble have I created thee…'" put in Brittany.

"How does Abdu'l-Bahá tell us to become noble?"

Jim groaned. "Act noble."

"Why isn't it noble to wear short skirts?" asked Anita, who had a body that almost any other girl in the room would have given her life savings to have.

Several students chuckled, and one boy said, "It may not be noble, but it's sure nice!"

With that comment, everybody laughed.

"Is it my fault that your thoughts aren't noble when you look at my short skirts? It seems like the problem's with the ones watching, not the ones wearing."

Many of the girls agreed loudly, but Jim spoke up.

"I can't believe I'm saying this, but if we're going to help lead people to God, we're not going to do it by tempting them and then telling them they shouldn't be being tempted."

"What do you suggest?" asked Zivar.

"We have to set the example and be so happy in being different that they ask us what gives."

"Ooo...Wisdom from Jim. That's surprising." Megan's words cut through, but the rest of the class understood that she was trying to save face, so they tolerated the comment without reacting to it.

"How can we be happy dressing weird?"

For the first time since the school year opened, Kavian had something to say, "It doesn't have to be weird. Maybe we could be like the football players. They wear ties to school the day of a game to show how important the game is to them. Maybe we should dress up more because school is important to us."

"Wow. That's scary," said Jim. "I think he might be making sense."

"If you think he's making sense, that is scary," said Zivar.

"Let's try it," said Brittany, who hated dressing up, and everyone knew it. She felt more comfortable hiding her body beneath sloppy, oversized clothes.

"Are you serious?" asked Megan.

"Yeah, I'm serious. We sit around here saying this is the most important time in the history of the entire earth, and complain about how no one knocks on our door and wants to become Bahá'ís. Once in a while we organize a teaching project or a service project, but for the most part, our religion is contained in Sunday morning Bahá'í classes, just like the society that's all around us.

"It seems to me that if we dress up every day for one week, kids will ask us what's going on. One of them might even be interested in hearing about the Faith. Others may laugh at us, but at least we wouldn't be alone, if everybody agrees to do it. And we'd draw attention to the Faith. Good attention. It's better than doing what we're doing now, which is nothing."

Not a sound could be heard as all of the students contemplated what drawing attention to themselves would mean. Teenagers generally prefer fitting in with their surroundings. Each generation has a need to be different, unique, independent; but through time, each generation has done those things as a unit, not as individuals.

"What does everyone think?" asked Mr. Jameson.

"I think it's crazy!" said Megan.

"Oh, come on, Megan," chided Jim. "You probably have less to lose than any of us."

"What?!!!"

He meant that she was the most popular of all the kids in the class, and therefore her actions would be more likely to start a new fad than to make her look ridiculous. But as soon as he saw her reaction, he knew that she thought he was referring back to the locker room scene and that her reputation was lost anyway. In an effort to find some way to explain, he considered a hundred quips, but nothing came to mind that might not be taken in another way, so he kept his mouth shut.

"Let's keep personalities out of this, shall we?" asked Mr. Jameson, casting a grimace towards Jim, who slumped deeper into his seat.

"Let's take a vote. All those in favor of giving dressing up for school a try for one week raise your hands."

Sixteen of the possible twenty-one raised their hands.

"Okay. Looks like we give it a try."

"Not me," said Megan.

"Hey, now, Megan," said Anita. "The Writings say if a vote can't be unanimous, everyone has to go with the majority. If I can do it, you can do it. It's only five days."

"What about the play?" returned Megan.

"This has nothing to do with the play. We're talking about what we wear on regular school days."

Megan looked around the room. "Fine," she said finally, without enthusiasm. "I'll do it."

Chapter Ten

Monday was to be the first entire run through of the play, complete with costumes, props, and scenery. It would no doubt be over after 11:00, and on a school night, that probably seemed crazy to anyone who wasn't in the production. But when each one of the cast members had been coming to rehearsals for over six weeks and had seen the play grow from a clumsy read-through to real characters living out the story on stage, nothing else mattered that week of performance, anyway. So what if there's a math test on Wednesday?

Ashley was caught up in the excitement. She had borrowed black jeans and a black turtleneck from one of the kids who had done scenery lots of times. She had even learned to move across the dark stage, unseen in her dark clothing, without tripping over anything, and that was no small accomplishment for her!

Last Wednesday when he had been driving her home from rehearsal, Greg had asked if she would help move sets. She had politely refused, explaining that her mother wouldn't let her stay out so late on a school night. When they had reached her house, without saying a word he got out of the car and walked up to her door with her.

"What are you doing?" she asked.

He just smiled at her and put his finger to his lips as if they shared a secret, which was silly, because she had no idea what the secret was.

"Hello, Mrs. O'Connor!" he greeted, "How are you doing this fine day?"

She laughed. She could see through Greg almost as easily as she could see through Ashley.

"And what is it you need from me 'this fine day,' Mr. Morrison?" she returned.

What Ashley couldn't understand was that he didn't seem embarrassed at all. He just joined in the laughter and said, "We need Ashley to help move sets for the play, but rehearsals next week will run late."

Mrs. O'Connor frowned. "When would she be able to get her homework done?"

Just as Ashley was beginning to think they were completely unaware of her presence, Greg turned to her and asked, "Do you think you could get it done after school? Dress rehearsals won't start until 6:30."

Ashley bit her lip. "I don't know. That's not much time."

"I can help you, if you want."

"Don't you have your own work?"

He shrugged. "I never sleep the week of a production. Too excited."

"Yeah, right."

"When would she eat dinner?" asked Mrs. O'Connor.

"Oh, there's always food around. People order pizza or bring stuff from home."

Seeing Mrs. O'Connor' face, he added, "I would be willing to take personal responsibility for making sure she eats some vegetables."

Ashley looked up at him with her hands on her hips.

"I can look after my own eating, thank you."

With a face filled with false innocence, he replied, "Ooo! All grown up just because we're turning sixteen in two weeks?"

Ashley's jaw dropped open.

"How did you know..."

"I have ways," he teased. Then turning to Mrs. O'Connor, he asked, "Well, do you think it would be all right?"

For several excruciating seconds, Mrs. O'Connor considered the issue. Qualifying her permission on discussion later with her husband, she finally said, "I guess we could try it once. If her grades suffer, we'll know not to do it again."

"Thank you! That'll be great!" exclaimed Greg. "I gotta get home. See you tomorrow, Ashley!"

And that was that. Now here she was, dressed all in black, standing back stage ready to dash on with the next flat. Life was weird.

As she watched Megan on stage, she became completely caught up in the make believe. Megan wasn't Megan anymore. She had become another person. Boys were interested in her— as many as she wanted. But, of course, the one she really wanted took the entire play to win over.

It was a life far removed from Ashley's, but probably not so far removed from Megan's or most other girls' at the high school, at least from where Ashley stood. It seemed to her that most of them had had lots of boyfriends by now. They worked hard to make themselves copies of the models in the teen magazines, and then knew they had done a good job when the right boy asked them out. Of course, the right boy this week was probably not going to be the right boy next week, but that was all part of the game.

Ashley had spent so much time envying them, that it made her jump with surprise when she realized that she was standing there feeling pity for all those girls. They thought that their faces and bodies were the most important aspects of themselves as human beings, and when the boys asked them out, it was a message sent that they were desirable, and therefore someone important. When they got older and their looks began to fade, they would think they weren't important anymore at all. Was there anything sadder than that?

"Yo, Ashley," Greg called in a stage whisper. "Wake up!"

She scrambled out onto the stage, lined up her end of the flat with its correct mark, then grabbed the small occasional table that needed to be taken off stage. All within ten seconds. The stage crew prided themselves on their speed.

"Where were you?" asked Greg.

Ashley smiled and hung her head. "You wouldn't believe me if I told you."

"Try me."

She opened her mouth, but Ms. Hillman's voice rang out from the back of the auditorium. "Quiet back stage!!"

On the way home, Greg asked, "You going to the cast party Saturday night?"

"No way."

"Why not?"

"I've heard that those things sometimes go on all night."

He thought for a moment. "I wish I could say that wasn't true, but I can't." He brightened. "There's never alcohol, though."

"Because the parties are always at Ms. Hillman's house, and she'd kill anyone who tried to smuggle in alcohol!"

"So? It's still not there."

She laughed. "I just don't think it would be my thing."

"I understand, but you don't know how hard it is to work on something for so long, have it be over, and then you have to go home. It's weird."

"That's my favorite word," she said, smiling.

He returned the smile and said, "I know."

There were those butterflies again! Ashley felt as if her entire stomach was doing flips.

"What if I had you home by midnight?" he asked, not wanting to let the subject drop.

"The play doesn't get over until 10:00! By the time everything gets cleaned up and put away, you wouldn't have time to enjoy the party at all before you'd have to drive me home!"

"This is my last year. I know there'll be a play next spring, but even so, it's important to me to at least make a showing."

"So go to the party!

As they pulled into the driveway, he brought the car to a stop and put it in park. Shutting off the engine, he turned to Ashley and said, "I don't want to go unless you go."

In her surprise, the word came out before she could grab onto it.

"Why?"

He turned away. "Do I have to spell out everything to you?! I told you weeks ago I was interested in you. I made a special effort to meet your mother. I made sure you always worked on the same flat I was working on, and I drive you home every day. How dumb can you be?!"

In a voice no louder than a whisper, she answered, "Pretty dumb."

Realizing what he had said, he hit his hand on the steering

wheel.

"Not as dumb as me, obviously," he said with contempt.

For the first time, she reached out and touched his arm.

"It's okay. I was being dumb, but when you look like me, you don't let actions that might mean something to someone else mean anything to you, because you know they can't."

"Why do you keep saying 'when you look like me?'"

"It doesn't take a high IQ to look into a mirror."

"Maybe you're comparing yourself to magazine faces instead of real people."

After considering his comment for a moment, she admitted, "Maybe."

"So how do I get through to you?" he asked, continuing to stare straight ahead.

"You already have gotten through to me."

With that, he turned to face her.

"Are you going to miss seeing me after school when we don't have rehearsal every day?"

"You know I will."

"No, I don't," he replied, reading for her chin with his right hand, gently forcing her to turn towards him. "That's why I'm asking."

For one brief instant, she looked into his eyes. "I can't even look at your face without feeling like I'm going to throw up."

He burst out laughing. "Now there's romance, if I ever heard it!"

"I didn't mean—" Her face was hot with embarrassment.

Touching her shoulder, he interrupted, "I know. It's okay, don't worry."

"I'm no good at this," she lamented.

"Neither am I."

"Oh, right. Like you've never dated before or anything!"

"Well, I've never been serious about anybody before."
Ashley drew her breath in so quickly, she started coughing, but he didn't stop there.
"Being with you is not like being with anybody else."
"I can believe that!" she added. By now, she feared she was near the point of giggling uncontrollably.
"Then why can't you believe that I really care for you?"
With the suddenness of a summer storm blown past, her laughter died.
At first she had no answer. She thought about what a kind, thoughtful person Greg was. It occurred to her that all boys might not be looking for a girl who was done up like the models in the magazines. And if there were guys like that, Greg would certainly be one of them. She knew she wouldn't necessarily be attracted to a boy just because he looked like the guys in those magazines, although in her estimation, Greg was better looking than any of the ones she had seen.
Then what was in the way?
She thought about all the times her parents had taught her to solve problems by identifying the spiritual problem involved.
Trust. That was it.
"Okay," she began, "even if I admit that I care about you, and you act like you care about me—"
"Thanks. It's not an act."
"I didn't say it was an act. I said from my point of view you act like someone who cares about me. Can I continue?"
"Sure."
"What you're really asking me to do is trust you. To trust the feelings that you say you have for me. But I'm new at this. I don't' know anything about how to tell if someone is playing games."
"Do you think I'm playing games with you?"

"No. Greg. I don't."

"Well. That's the most positive thing you've said so far."

"Give me time."

"Sure. Fine. Okay."

She took another deep breath as if it would give her more strength to continue. "If two people are going to be serious about each other, they have to get to know each other as well as they can. They have to test their feelings with time, work through disagreements, work through how they each feel about really important things. Would you agree with that?"

"Completely."

"Oh...Well, if you want to have a serious response to a comment like you've 'never been serious about anybody before,' you have to be willing to commit yourself to taking the time to put your feelings to the test."

"That's what I've been trying to get through to you all along. I'm willing. I'm willing! But are you?"

In something she imagined was close to shock, she gasped, "Haven't I just said that I am?"

"No, you haven't."

With all the courage she could muster, Ashley looked into Greg's eyes and said, "Then I can't think of anything I'd rather spend time doing."

He grabbed her hand, cried out, "All right!" and bent as if to kiss her, but then leaned back, took in a deep breath, and said, "If I were any happier, I'd explode."

Chapter Eleven

As Brittany walked into her geometry class on Tuesday, Mr. Kelly looked up and smiled.

"Dressing up two days in a row?" he asked. "What's the occasion? New boyfriend?"

"Oh, yeah. That's it. New boyfriend," she replied with a chuckle. She always seemed to be more at ease with adults than with kids her own age.

"So, what's the deal?"

"We decided at Bahá'í school Sunday that we'd dress up for school to make it seem more important. You know, people dress up for things that are important to them."

"I like the thought. I wish you could get some of the other kids to dress up. Not fancy, really, just like their clothes weren't ten sizes too big."

"They're just more comfortable that way." Brittany couldn't believe she was defending some of the very students she thought were ridiculous, with the way they wore their pants like they would fall off any minute. Maybe it was because she liked clothes that hid her body, even though that had nothing to do with present fads.

"Probably so. What's Bahá'í school, anyway?"

"We are Bahá'ís. That's our religion. We're not exactly Christians, but Sunday mornings are just convenient for people to get together."

Ryoko had been listening to the conversation.

"What do you mean by 'not exactly Christians'?" she asked.

All of a sudden, Brittany realized that several of the students around her were listening to the discussion. Words generally came easily to her, but she had a feeling that this particular answer might be the most important one she had ever given in her life.

After a short hesitation, she explained, "We believe that Jesus was the Son of God, so it's not like we are lowering His station, but we also believe that there were other Manifestations who were just as important as Jesus was."

"That's crazy," said someone, but Brittany couldn't see who it was.

Hurriedly, she continued, "Well, the best thing about it is that I can walk up to a Jew and honestly say that I think his or her religion is just as valid as my own. Since religion is such a personal thing, I feel more comfortable with that than having to tell someone that they have to agree with me or go to hell."

"Oooo! Mr. Kelly, are you going to let her get away with that language?"

"For heaven's sake, Jackson, she was talking about the place, not telling anyone to go there."

Several students laughed, but Ryoko leaned closer to Brittany to ask, "What about Buddha?"

"Sure. Buddha was one of the Manifestations of God."

"I'm a Buddhist," she whispered.

"Cool!" replied Brittany, and as Ryoko returned her smile, Mr. Kelly started the class on the day's new theorem. After class, Ryoko caught up with Brittany in the hall.

"I didn't know there was anyone around here who believed Buddha was more than just a nice man."

"There are about thirty high school kids in the area who are Bahá'í s, I think, but only six here. Our religion is really new as religions go."

"New? Don't you just accept all religions?"

"Now that's a hard question. The correct answer is yes and no. Yes, we accept all major religions—there are certain criteria. We don't acknowledge cult leaders and stuff like that."

Brittany was used to pausing for comments by anyone she was having a conversation with, but Ryoko was just looking at her, patiently waiting for her to continue.

"Okay. The no part is that we don't JUST accept other religions. We follow the specific teachings of a Manifestation called Bahá'u'lláh, which translates as the "Glory of God." He lived from 1817 to 1892. That's why our religion is so new."

"What makes His teachings different? Besides accepting other religions, of course."

"All the Manifestations had the same spiritual teachings, but different social teachings for the time in which they appeared. Bahá'u'lláh gave us the special message for our time."

Ryoko stopped where a second hallway turned off to the right.

"I have to go to English," she said. "But do you think you could tell me more about this…Baha?"

She couldn't quite say it, so Brittany helped her.

"Bahá'u'lláh."

"Bahá'u'lláh," repeated Ryoko. "Thanks. Could you tell me

more sometime?"

"Sure. That would be great!"

Brittany couldn't believe it! As Ryoko walked down the hall away from her, she realized that she had actually taught the Faith! Just because they had decided to dress up this week! Even if no one became a Bahá'í, it felt good to know that more people knew something about it because of her.

"Cool," she thought.

In gym class, she tried to tell Megan about it, but Megan was preoccupied with something, and virtually ignored her. Unfortunately, Brittany's temper was almost as short as Megan's, and she nearly decided to walk away and ignore Megan completely. But then she remembered a thought she had had about wanting to be more like Ashley. Ashley would try to think of a reason why Megan was acting so distant.

The play, of course. How could she have been so stupid? Megan was probably exhausted from the late rehearsals this week. And maybe even Megan, the star actress, was getting a little nervous.

"How's the play going?" she asked.

Megan looked at her as if seeing her for the first time that day.

"Oh, hi, Brittany. The play? It's going fine."

Boy, she really was distracted, thought Brittany. Out loud, she said, "You look tired."

Megan blinked her eyes as if trying to stay focused on the conversation. "Yeah, I guess I am."

It was not like Megan to be vague. She usually said exactly what was on her mind.

Tentatively, Brittany asked, "Is anything wrong?"

Too quickly, Megan answered, "Of course not! Don't be silly! Everything's fine!

I'm just a little tired, that's all. No big deal!"

"Okay! Okay! Sorry I asked!"

Nothing more was said, but Brittany could not help herself from thinking about how concerned Ashley had been lately about Megan. Ashley was in tune with such things, but Brittany figured Megan must be pretty bad off if even she, Brittany, could see that something was wrong.

Chapter Twelve

After school Wednesday, Megan walked into the auditorium for rehearsal. The cast was just supposed to review weak spots today and take a night off before the performances Thursday, Friday, and Saturday. Kevin was already there, and as Megan entered, he walked over to her.

"You've sure been lookin' good this week—not that you don't always, but you've been dressing up. Are you trying to drive me crazy, or what?" he asked.

"Don't flatter yourself. All of the Bahá'í s are dressing up this week."

"All of the what?"

"Bahá'ís. That's our religion."

"I never heard of it, but I like it."

"What makes you say that?"

"Because it made you dress up this week, and I like the way I feel when I look at you all dressed up."

"You're crazy."

"Crazy about you."

Megan laughed. Kevin could always make her laugh, it seemed. Maybe being around him just made her happy. That wasn't such a bad thing.

"It's like another part you play," Kevin continued.

"What do you mean?"

"You look all prim and proper. You'd turn the head of any guy that saw you, but I'm the one who gets to kiss you. I'm the one who knows the real you."

"What makes you think you know the real me?" she returned somewhat indignantly. "You know who I am on stage, that's all."

"Yeah, right. And I know who you are back in the hallways, too. You're mine."

She thought she should be offended at that, but he put his arm around her and pulled her close, and she felt that giddy feeling come over her again. He only kissed her forehead (they were in public after all), but at that moment, Megan thought that kissing her forehead was much more romantic than a real kiss would have been.

"He really does care about me!" she thought. "It's not just the play!"

As he gently pulled away, she reached for his hand and brought it to her own lips. He seemed surprised. That was the effect she wanted.

Out loud she said, "I gotta get ready."

"We're not wearing costumes today," he said, not wanting her to go.

"I know, but there's a couple of props I need backstage."

"Hurry back!" he called after her.

From somewhere else in the auditorium, she overheard one of the other cast members say, "Look at that. He can't stand to be away from her even for a minute."

Megan felt a warm glow inside. She had captured the heart of the cutest boy in school.

Ashley had been watching the entire scene. Even though she couldn't hear what was being said, she saw the way Megan and Kevin looked at each other. Turning to Greg, she said, "Maybe Kevin's intentions are honorable after all."

"I wish I could say that I thought so."

"Do you think he's leading her on?"

"Not really. I'm pretty sure he enjoys being with her, but his idea of what a high school relationship involves is different from hers, I'll bet."

"You mean like that magazine I told you about where a boy said that having sex was part of the process of getting to know a girl?"

"Yeah. And he's not the only one who thinks so. I wouldn't be surprised if most guys felt that way."

"Why shouldn't they if they can get away with it?"

Greg stared at her. "I can't believe you said that!"

"I didn't say I agreed with it! But as long as there are plenty of girls around who are willing to go along with them, they have no reason to think differently."

"I disagree! It takes two people to have sex, and I think the responsibility for saying no rests on both of them, not just the girl."

"You mean that even if the girl is willing, the boy should say no?"

"Of course!"

Ashley giggled. "You know, you're right, but I don't see it happening any time soon."

"History hasn't exactly been a good model."

"You've heard the saying 'boys will be boys.'"

"Yeah, and I think that's letting us off too easy."

"I guess it relieves guys of any responsibility, doesn't it?"

"Of course! If they do something inappropriate, they excuse it by saying they were just being normal, healthy boys."

"This is kind of a weird thought..." began Ashley.

"You think a lot of your thoughts are weird," he laughed.

She hit him affectionately on the shoulder.

"What I was going to say before I was so rudely interrupted—"

"Oh! Excuse me!"

Ashley opened her eyes wide as she hit him again, not quite so affectionately. "I was trying to say that if we humans are here to acquire spiritual qualities, we are really crippling the progress of *males* by having that attitude."

"I see your point, but I don't think they feel very crippled by it. I think they would see it as a sort of freedom."

"You mean, do what you want, no consequences?"

"Yep. I've also known that somehow society expects girls to stay pure and guys to get experience before they commit to marriage, although how anybody believes that, I'll never know!" Greg shook his head at society's twisting of values.

Ashley agreed, "Really. It does take two, like you said. But how do we change attitudes?"

"Don't buy into it, I guess. Parents probably have the most effect. If they raise their sons to be responsible instead of what is currently accepted as 'typical,' that would make a difference."

"The Bahá'í Writings say that the mother has the most influence over the morality of her children when they are really young. They say kids are like young trees that will grow in any direction you train them."

"Well, our children will be in good shape, then."

Ashley was so embarrassed she couldn't speak.

"Sorry. I didn't mean to upset you. I thought we were supposed to be talking about important things, and I figured raising kids counted."

"I—It does," she managed to stammer. "I just wasn't expecting it."

"I like thinking about being married to you."

Again, Ashley could not answer.

"Maybe I'm not being fair," he said, looking away. "I'm eighteen and nearly finished with high school. Even though I'm planning on college, it's easy for me to think about settling down. You're just beginning to date."

Ashley watched his face as he appeared to be studying his shoes. Without planning to at all, she found herself saying, "I don't think Bahá'ís really date. In fact, there's one letter written on behalf of Shoghi Effendi where one might even interpret it to mean that we're encouraged to marry young to help us channel our natural desires."

"No kidding?"

"No kidding."

"How young?"

Swallowing hard, realizing that there was probably no way to avoid the inevitable, Ashley still tried to answer the question in generalities.

"Bahá'u'lláh set the age of maturity for marriage, but I really think He was talking about further in the future."

"Why? What age did He say?"

Ashley was committed now. In a voice that was barely audible, she whispered, "Fifteen."

Now it was Greg's turn to be speechless. But after several seconds, he let out a loud, "Wahoo!" causing Ms. Hillman to turn and glare at him.

"We're working here, Mr. Morrison, if you didn't notice," she said. "I'll get to the notes for improving scene changes in a minute, but please be more respectful of others."

"I'm sorry, Ms. Hillman. I just heard some amazing news."

"You want to interrupt rehearsal to share it with everyone?" Greg smiled. He and Ms. Hillman had had a great working relationship for years.

"No thanks," he answered.

"That's what I thought," she said, glancing fondly at Ashley before she turned back around to get back to work. She didn't really understand what Greg saw in the girl, but she had complete confidence in his judgment.

She thought, "There must be more to her than I can tell on the outside," and then chuckled at herself for coming up with such a trite thought. Of course there was more to the girl than one could tell from the outside!

Chapter Thirteen

Dear Diary,

I can't believe it's been over a week since I wrote in here! I guess I've been busy with all of the rehearsals for the play. Well, to be honest, I've spent a lot of time with Greg. That sounds funny. He's so much a part of my life, and we've only know each other for a couple of months.

This afternoon he said that he liked thinking about being married to me! I couldn't believe it! I mean, it's not like he asked me to marry him or anything. But doesn't it mean something when someone says they like thinking about being married to you?

I can't imagine being married to such a cute guy. People would look at us like he was crazy to want someone like me. You know what's funny, though? When I'm with him, I almost feel pretty. He never looks at me like he feels sorry for me. He looks at me like...like he cares about what I think. Almost like he wants to learn from me, as if I have some secret that he wants to share.

Weird.

I think Kevin really likes Megan. Greg says he doesn't think it's real love, more like lust, but I'm not so sure. He always wants to be with her, holding her hand, putting his arm around her...He's not embarrassed to let other people know he likes her. That must mean something! Maybe everything's going to be all right with them. I just wish I could get rid of the feeling that all that touching isn't healthy. It leads to other things, and with the way she dresses for the play, it doesn't exactly tell him no.

Even Brittany's worried, and she doesn't usually notice things like that. You know, she's gotten quieter in the last couple of weeks. I wonder if everything's okay with her. I'm going to try to talk with her tomorrow during lunch.

See ya later,

Ashley

On Thursday, Ashley found Brittany in the hallway outside the cafeteria. She had her lunch with her in a paper bag, which was unusual because Brittany ate school lunch almost every day.

"Hey, Brittany, how's it going?" called Ashley.

Looking up as if awakened from a dream, Brittany looked around, finally focusing on Ashley.

"Oh, hi, Ashley. What's up with you?"

"No fair, I asked you first!" Ashley replied, laughing.

"Yeah, I guess you did."

As Brittany returned the smile, Ashley noticed that it had been awhile since she had seen her friend happy. The thought made her frown.

"What's wrong?" Brittany asked.

"I just had the feeling that it had been awhile since I saw you smiling. Are you okay?"

"Everything's peachy," replied Brittany without enthusiasm. But Ashley was not as easily put off as Brittany's mom, who had never been comfortable with talking about inner feelings. She sat looking at her friend with all the patience of a Buddha.

"Okay," gave in Brittany. "You win. Mom's just made some comments about my self-centeredness lately. It's like she thinks it's my only quality."

"You have a lot of wonderful qualities! That's silly!"

"Thanks, but sometimes…"

As her voice trailed off, Ashley interjected, "Don't you dare believe it! You're smart, and pretty, and you help me whenever I need it. That's important! And you're not self-centered, you're self-confident. There's a difference!"

Brittany smiled at her friend. "You always make me feel better, Ashley." She took a bite of her red apple. "I've been worried that you wouldn't have time for me anymore now that you've gotten into…the drama club. You seem busy all of the time."

"I am busy all of the time! But after this week is over, my life will be more sane again."

"You're not going to do the winter play?"

"No way. I've got to concentrate on my studies."

"Yeah, right. I sort of had the idea that you would be going to a lot of basketball games this year."

Ashley flushed beet red.

"W-why should I want to go to basketball games?"

Brittany laughed. "Oh, Ashley, don't you know that the whole school has noticed who you ride home with every night? I'm never at the practices, and we hardly have time to talk anymore, but I still know all about it!"

The thought that anyone had been paying attention to her being with Greg had never really occurred to Ashley. She imagined theirs a private world.

"In all honesty," Brittany continued, "I thought he was just after you for—for physical reasons, he being a jock and all. But I was talking to Ryoko yesterday, and her brother, Shunsuke is in the same Government class as Greg."

"Who's Ryoko?" asked Ashley.

"Oh! That's another story I have to tell you! But let me finish this one first, okay?"

"Okay."

"Anyway, Shunsuke said that someone—I think she said his name was Jeff—was giving Greg a hard time about driving you home every night…Stuff like did he really have to date someone that ugly to find a virgin, and Greg nearly knocked his head off! Shunsuke said it took three guys to hold Greg off from him!"

Ashley was horrified and flattered at the same time. After all, she had been called ugly before, but it was never fun to hear. On the other hand, she had never had anyone stick up for her before. Well, that wasn't fair. Nobody besides her parents or Brittany…certainly not a guy. It was a nice feeling even if she wasn't fond of fighting.

"Was anybody hurt?" she asked.

"No, lucky for Jeff the other three held Greg off. When Greg finally settled down enough for them to let him go, all he said was that he didn't think Jeff would know a real woman if he saw one. Isn't that cool?"

"It's a lot better than cool. I don't even know what to say. He didn't mention it at practice yesterday at all. In fact" She stopped, guilt spreading across her face for what she had almost said.

"Ashley, what did he say yesterday at practice? C'mon! You can tell me!"

"No, it's too private."

"Did he tell you that he loved you?"

"No! But I said it was too private!"

"What do you mean too private? I thought we were best friends."

The last thing Ashley wanted to do was hurt Brittany's feelings, but some things *were* too private, even for a best friend. What could she tell Brittany to make her feel included without betraying any confidences of Greg?

"Well," she began, "he was just talking about this being his last year of high school, and you know, even going on to college, life will never be the same..."

"So what did that have to do with you?"

An idea struck Ashley. "Nothing really. That's why I didn't want to make it sound like it meant anything. But he did ask me about my plans for the future. Like it was important to him. I thought maybe—"

"Definitely! I'd say it definitely means he intends to continue your relationship after the play is over!"

"Well," replied Ashley, hoping to not look too relieved, "that's what I was hoping it might mean."

"Gee, Ashley, that's so cool!" beamed Brittany.

"Thanks," replied Ashley. "I think so, too. But I better get to class before the bell rings."

"Me, too," said Brittany. But as she watched Ashley hurry away, she couldn't help being a little jealous. If some guy could look past Ashley's plain face and see Ashley's good qualities, why couldn't some guy look past her size? She had a pretty face, she knew. That was her best feature. And it wasn't as if Greg were some nerd or anything. He had been elected

Homecoming King, for heaven's sake! Why was it that Ashley could interest one of the most popular boys in high school, and she couldn't interest any boy at all? Life wasn't fair. Maybe it was because she didn't have any good qualities to find. She enjoyed being smart, and it made most guys really uncomfortable. She was often the one who figured out how something should be done, but it was only because her ideas were usually right. It wasn't her fault she was so smart. What did they want her to do? Pretend she was dumb?

Maybe her mother was right. Maybe she was just self-centered.

Great. Brittany hated days like today.

Chapter Fourteen

Megan didn't bother to go home Friday after school. She had to be back by six o'clock for make-up anyway, and running around before a show made her more nervous. As they had done in the past, her parents would take her out for a fancy meal the day after the last show, but beforehand, she preferred to just eat some salad or fruit and be alone.

She wandered into the greenroom, and was surprised to see Ashley there. The fact that she had seen her could not be denied, so she tried to be at least civil.

"Hello, Ashley."

"Hi, Megan. Good luck tonight."

"Oh, you should never wish an actress good luck before a performance! It's bad luck! You should say, 'Break a leg.'"

"Oh, sorry! I didn't realize—"

"Forget it. It's no big deal."

"Nothing is."

"What's that supposed to mean?"

"You just say that a lot, that's all," Ashley defended hastily. "I didn't mean anything by it."

"Yeah, okay. Whatcha doin'?"

"With this schedule, I have to do homework anytime I can find a spare minute. I don't see how you do it! This week has been crazy, and I'm not under half the pressure you are!" Megan tried to sound as experienced as she could. "You get used to it."

Ashley sat, looking up at Megan, wondering what she could say to get things back to where they used to be before the day they had 'bumped into each other' in the hallway. Finally, she looked down to the floor and said, "Look, Megan, I'm sorry if I said anything that hurt your feelings."

When Megan didn't reply, Ashley looked up at her. Megan's jaw was clenched as tightly as her fist. By the way she was blinking, Ashley knew Megan was fighting back tears.

"What is it? What's the matter, Megan?"

Biting her lip, Megan answered, "Before that day, I felt really in control of my life—as much as anyone can, anyway. I knew what was in fashion, I knew what should be said or done in certain circumstances, I knew how to make a boy take a second look.

"I knew how to play the game with parents! As long as they didn't find out you were doing something, it was okay to do it.

"Then you made that comment about having no secrets from God. Now I feel like I have this ghost following me around, watching everything I do. It's awful!"

Megan started pacing whenever she was emotional about something, and at this rate, she was going to wear a hole in the carpet.

"I can't relax! Every time I go to do something, I have to stop and think, 'God can see me. What would He want me to do?'"

In an effort to ease Megan's pain, Ashley said, "But why is that bad? It's good to have God with you every day! Religion is a way of life, not a Sunday morning activity!"

Megan stopped pacing. Her eyes seemed to drill into Ashley's.

"I hate it! God wants me to be perfect, and I can't be perfect. I was happier before."

Ashley didn't know what to say. She wished someone with more brains were here to help. But there wasn't anyone with more brains around. If anyone were going to help Megan, it had to be her.

"Look, Megan," she began. "I don't have any answers. But I can't believe you were really happier before. Bahá'u'lláh said that human happiness comes from spiritual behavior, remember?"

Megan made no reply, so Ashley continued.

"All humans have a spiritual side and a material side. The material part is just while we live here, but the spiritual part is the real us. The material part can feel happy, but it's just as temporary as our lives in this world. Real happiness is when our spirits are happy."

"For somebody who says she's dumb, you sure have a lot of answers."

Ashley looked up at the ceiling and then closed her eyes to keep from crying. "They're not my answers, Megan. You know that."

"But you make it sound so easy!"

"Life is never easy."

"Well, how do we know when our spirits are happy?!"

"I don't know!" She sat for a moment, and then had an idea. "Maybe it's a kind of fullness. When only your material part is happy, there's a need for more. You know, like when people do drugs or drink to try to get higher or fill some empty part of themselves.

"But when your spirit is happy, you feel full. There's not a driving need to keep searching because you've found what you need."

Megan slumped down on the couch.

"I haven't found anything."

Looking directly at Megan, Ashley said, "I think you have. Wouldn't it be great if you thought God could see you all the time, but He was happy with what He saw?"

"That could never happen!"

"Of course it could! You know what makes God happy!"

"If I live like Shoghi Effendi describes in *The Advent of Divine Justice*, I'll never have a social life!"

"Of course you will! It just won't be like it was before."

"I felt more comfortable then."

"I don't believe that."

"He wants us to be perfect!"

"He wants us to try our best to acquire spiritual qualities. God knows we can't be perfect. He loves us anyway."

Tears trickled down Megan's cheeks. She didn't sob; she didn't cry out. But as she looked down at the floor, the drops of salty water found their way down her lovely face and dropped off onto her crossed arms.

Ashley was a little frightened by the silence. When Megan was pacing and ranting about something, at least Ashley knew what was going on in her mind. Now there was no way to tell.

"Megan?"

No response.

"Megan? Listen. If you're worried about the play, God gave you a talent for acting. It's a gift from Him. It's a good thing."

Slowly, Megan raised her head to look at Ashley.

"That doesn't make any sense. Acting is bad."

"No it isn't! It's the Hollywood kind of acting that's bad. You know, 'R' rated stuff."

"What do you think about this play?"

By not answering right away, Ashley made her thoughts clear enough, even though all she said was, "I don't know."

"So do you think I shouldn't go on tonight?"

"You're the only one who can answer that, but I can't see what purpose it would serve by letting the entire cast and crew down. I think the time for deciding is before you take a part."

"So it's too late?"

"If Bahá'u'lláh were standing here, what do you think He would want you to do?"

Megan closed her eyes and thought for a moment.

"Do the show, but never take a part like this again."

"Then that's what you should do!"

"Ashley, there aren't many parts out there that Bahá'u'lláh would approve of."

"So it's a market with lots of growth potential!"

Megan burst out laughing, and Ashley joined her. As they hugged each other, Megan said, "I still have a lot of thinking to do, you know."

"Great! Just don't forget the praying part."

At that moment, Greg poked his head in the door.

"Ashley? Hey! You two finally made up!"

Megan started wiping at her eyes, and Greg handed her his handkerchief. "Yeah, I guess so. It's hard to stay mad at Ashley," she said.

"I feel the same way," replied Greg, putting his arm affectionately around Ashley's shoulders.

"You guys are weird," said Ashley, and they all laughed.

Chapter Fifteen

The performance of the play went well, and when Megan laid down on her bed to go to sleep, her mind was still spinning with thoughts about everything that had been happening lately. The audience had called her out for two extra curtain calls with Kevin. That was nearly unheard of in a high school production, and Megan felt that it wasn't really fair of God to give her a talent that had no market. Being on stage felt as natural to her as getting good grades was to Brittany. Didn't that count for something? But if she went on to Broadway or Hollywood, she knew she would be expected to do a lot of things that Bahá'u'lláh wouldn't like.

We're supposed to excel at what we do, she thought. Why should acting be any different? Ashley's words of that afternoon came back to her. It wasn't the acting that was bad, it was what they did with it in places like Hollywood. But where could an actress make a living that wouldn't be against what Bahá'u'lláh taught? In a restaurant, that's where. Waiting tables.

Welcome to the real world.

If God wanted us to be happy, He sure had a funny way of showing it. And what about Kevin? She liked the way he made her feel...pretty, wanted, really special. She was pretty sure that he would want to continue their relationship after the play, and that sounded good to her. What was wrong with a Bahá'í having the cutest guy in the school for a boyfriend? Look at Ashley and Greg.

But as soon as Megan thought about Ashley and Greg, she knew what the difference was between their relationship and hers with Kevin. She knew they would never be caught in the hallway kissing. But wasn't that a bit extreme? Everyone expected high school couples to do some things. There were a lot of kids that had sex and thought it was no big deal.

Why did God make it such a big deal, and then give teens, especially guys, such a need for having sex? It didn't make sense. Maybe Bahá'ís were missing something in their interpretation of the Writings...

After the play Saturday night, everyone scurried around breaking sets quickly so they could get to the cast party. Kevin waited outside the girls' dressing room for Megan.

She finally came out, laden with costumes and bags of accessories. When she saw him, she said, "Where's all your stuff?"

"I put it in the trunk already. I figured that you'd need help carrying stuff."

Megan smiled warmly. "That's nice! Thanks!"

"My pleasure, Madam!" he replied, bowing graciously before relieving her of most of her load.

"Mademoiselle, if you please!" she corrected with mock

indignity, and they trooped out to Kevin's car and loading her things in the back seat.

"Do you want to drop this stuff by your house before the party? That way you won't have to worry about it when you're more tired."

"That would be great!" said Megan.

As they drove out to her house, she looked at Kevin. He really was handsome, she thought. And he was being so considerate this evening! Most people assumed that if a high school boy was handsome and popular, he was stuck up and had bad manners. But she didn't think Kevin fit into that mold at all.

They had dropped off her things and headed on to the party when Kevin took a different road than Megan expected.

"Is this a short cut?" she asked.

He flashed her a wonderful smile.

"Of course!"

But soon they were obviously out in the middle of nowhere, and Kevin parked and turned off the engine. Megan's stomach began to feel about like it felt before the curtain goes up on opening night, but she wasn't about to let him know she was nervous. She looked him straight in the eye and said, "I thought we were going to the party."

"We are! We are! I just thought it might be nice to take a little detour first," he said as he moved closer to her.

Megan enjoyed kissing Kevin, but when he started getting bolder, she pushed him away.

He looked confused. "What's going on?"

She dodged the issue by saying, "I think we're going to be missed if we don't go on to the party."

He smiled. "Oh, it'll be okay. We can just say that we drove by your house first. It's not a lie." And he bent to kiss her again.

Leaning to the right to give herself space, Megan said, "They know how long it takes to get to my house. We shouldn't add any more to the extra time we've already taken."

Now he was getting angry. As he sat back against his own seat, he accused, "What are you doing? Just teasing me? Leading me on? I didn't think you were like that."

"I'm not like that!" Megan defended. "I really do care about you."

"Not as much as I thought, evidently."

"What, because I won't let you touch me anywhere you want, you think I don't care enough?!"

"In a word, yes! A girl who really cares about a guy likes to please him."

Turning towards her window, Megan asked, "Is that the only way I can please you?"

"Not the *only* way, but it's a good start."

"Start?!" Her eyes flashed as she whipped around to face him again.

"Yeah, start. It gets better, you know." With a sudden look of surprise, he added, "You *don't* know, do you?"

"Don't know what?"

"Are you a virgin?!"

"Hey! What business is that of yours?"

"Well, the way you acted, I thought you…Never mind. I didn't realize. Gosh, I haven't been with a virgin for a long time." He was the epitome of gentleness, and it made her burn with anger. "Don't worry, Megan, I can be more patient with you. We can wait awhile."

Even in her anger, Megan was a smart young lady, and finding an opportunity, she jumped at it.

"Oh, Kevin, thank you! I'm only fifteen, you know. I think I need a little more time. Could we go to the party now?"

"Sure, Babe, whatever you say. I guess I can keep up with the cold showers for a couple more weeks."

She kissed him lightly on the cheek.

"You're really good to me," she cooed.

"Thanks. You'll get your chance to be really good to me soon."

She didn't say a word as they drove on to the party. The phrase "the way you acted" kept ringing in her brain. At first, her reaction was to say 'no big deal,' and forget about it. But somewhere inside her an alarm was sounding. Kevin had made it perfectly clear how far he expected their relationship to go, and she wasn't entirely convinced that it *was* no big deal. There was no doubt in her mind what the Writings said on the subject, and Megan knew this was a decision she had to make now.

On one hand, if she told him no forever, she would definitely lose him. Of that she had no doubt. He would also waste no time telling everyone in school that she was a scared little virgin who didn't understand the score. No one would ask her out then!

Hey! But how did that compare with him telling the whole school that she wasn't a scared little virgin? What kind of guys would ask her out then? No mystery there.

Of course, she might just stay with Kevin through high school and then marry him. That would be okay, wouldn't it?

Yeah, right. And they would go off to a castle and live happily ever after.

She sighed. Marriage was about as far away from Kevin's mind as being a monk was, and he was definitely not attracted to that! For that matter, she wasn't sure she cared enough for Kevin to think about marriage.

What was she saying?! Marriage??!! She was only fifteen!! She wanted to go places and do exciting things, get through college and live in a foreign country for a while. Marriage??!! That was crazy!

As they pulled over to park as close as they could to Ms. Hillman's house, Kevin turned to Megan.

"You've been awful quiet. I'm sorry if I scared you before. Are you going to be all right?" he asked.

"Funny you should ask that question," she answered. "I think I'm going to be just fine, thanks. Because I've figured out..." She stopped as an idea occurred to her. With a devilish twinkle in her eye, she continued. "I figured out that you must really love me if you want to think about marriage when we're so young."

"What?!"

"Didn't you mean before that you wanted to have sex with me?" she asked with all the innocence she could muster.

"Well, yeah, but I didn't say anything about marriage..."

"Of course you did! You can't have sex without marriage, everybody knows that! I just feel so lucky! Mrs. Megan Bradley! Doesn't that sound perfect!? I can't wait to tell everybody at the party—"

"Now wait a minute! You can't tell anyone that I want to marry you!"

Keeping her innocent composure, she asked, "But why not, Silly? Something that wonderful shouldn't be kept a secret!"

She leaned towards him as if to put her arms around him, but he opened his car door and stumbled out onto the ground as he tried to get away from her.

"But, Kevin, *Darling*, what's wrong?" she asked.

"I never said anything about m-m-marriage! I'm too young for something like that!"

Without saying a word, she got out of the car on her own side. Then, looking him straight in the eye, she said, "Then you're too young to have sex."

"I don't know what planet you're from, but I just wanted to

have a little fun! That's all!"

"That's what I thought, Bozo! But you'll have to get your *fun* somewhere else, because I don't want to miss out on all *my* fun by getting stuck raising a rug rat of yours from some stupid *accident!*"

Anger was starting to bubble up through his shock.

"Do you think I don't *know* how to be careful?" he asked indignantly.

"Don't you *know* that no birth control is a hundred percent effective? The only way to be careful is not to have sex until you're ready for kids, and for me that comes with marriage, and I'm not interested in marrying you!"

Megan turned and stomped off towards the party leaving Kevin with his mouth hanging open in disbelief. As she disappeared into the house, all he could think to do was slam his car door, but it didn't give him much satisfaction.

Chapter Sixteen

At the party, Megan fought through the crowd as she looked for Ashley. People were congratulating her, and she tried to be gracious, but her frustration was increasing. Finally, she called out, "Does anybody know where Ashley is?!"

Most of the kids just looked at her in surprise. Ashley was not popular at all. They knew there was some sort of connection—Megan and Ashley went to the same church or something—but that didn't explain why Megan wanted to find Ashley at a cast party where Megan should be the center of attention. On the other hand, people who played the lead parts often got rather melancholy after a show was over. Maybe Megan was just being sentimental about something.

"She and Greg left just a minute ago," returned someone.

"Oh, no!"

Megan pushed her way back through the crowd to the front door. When she saw Greg standing there, she said, "Oh, thank God you're still here!"

He took one look at her face and said, "What is it? What's wrong?"

"Where's Ashley?"

"She went back to get the dish she brought cookies in. What's up?"

Megan turned around, saw Ashley approaching, and ran to her. "Can you take me home? Please?" she asked.

"What's wrong?"

"I'll tell you in the car, but could you guys please get me out of here?"

"Of course," said Greg, and he guided both girls out the door and over to his car.

As he opened the door, he looked across the yard and noticed Kevin crossing toward the house. He was definitely not a happy camper.

"Uh-oh. I have a feeling I know what's wrong," he said.

Megan climbed into the back seat and replied, "Is it so obvious? Couldn't you at least let me make a good story out of it?"

Quickly sharing what had happened, Megan seemed to relax. Having someone there she knew would be sympathetic helped her deal with the situation she had just been through. When she got to the part about Kevin falling out of the car in an effort to get away from her, she even started giggling. Greg began laughing, too. Ashley tried to focus on her sympathy for her friend, but couldn't help saying, "I wish I could have seen that!" and joined the laughter.

By the time they pulled up in front of Megan's house, she was feeling much better. She got out of the car, and said, "Thanks, you guys. I don't know what I would have done without you! I think I played a good part in front of Kevin, but inside, I was shaking like a leaf!"

"I'm just glad you're safe!" said Ashley.

"Yeah, me too. Although I don't think my reputation is very safe!"

Greg shook his head. "I don't agree," he said. "Think of what your reputation would have been if you hadn't fought him off."

"Oh, I don't know," replied Megan. As Ashley and Greg stared at her in shock, she added, "Don't look at me like that. I just meant that I could have been more gentle with him. He would have left me alone tonight, and then I could have broken up with him before he had another chance."

"That's too dangerous," said Greg.

"I agree," added Ashley. "I think you did the right thing." She looked straight into Megan's eyes and said, "In fact, I'm sure you did the right thing. Don't you feel happy?"

She emphasized the last word, and Megan chuckled.

"As a matter of fact, I do. But I'd better go in now. It's after midnight, and I'm tired."

"Oh, gosh! After midnight?" Ashley asked with alarm.

"Yes, why?"

Greg made a face. "I told her parents I'd have her home by midnight."

"Don't worry. I'll call them as soon as I get inside. If I just allude to why I had you bring me home, I think they'll understand."

"Thanks, Megan," replied Ashley. "You're a great friend!"

This time it was Megan's turn to look surprised. She had been told she was beautiful; she had been told she was smart. She had been told she was talented, but she couldn't remember anyone telling her she was a great friend.

With all the awe of a newfound part of life, she whispered, "Thanks," and walked slowly up to her door.

Ashley was quiet on the way home.

After several minutes, Greg asked, "Are you okay?"

"Yeah. That was just too close for my comfort."

"Megan's tough. She came through all right."

"I know. I'm glad she's so smart. I could never think of all those things to say."

"Thinking of things to say is one of Megan's fortes. The problem is that too often she says things without thinking."

"That's enough," Ashley gently chided. "She had a major triumph tonight."

"I know. I'm sorry. But anyway, I'll make sure you never have to think of things like that to say."

"Yeah, right. Are you going to come back and watch over me when you're away at school next year?"

"Of course! Every week-end!"

Ashley laughed, but Greg frowned.

"Don't you believe me?"

She could tell his feelings were a little hurt, so she answered with all seriousness. "I believe that I'll never have to say those words to you. And I believe that you're the most amazing man I've ever met. But college changes people, Greg. There's no way you can stop it, and you shouldn't even try. You should grow as you learn. So let's just take one day at a time."

Stopping the car in her driveway, he replied, "Very wise, young lady. But you're missing one piece."

"What do you mean?"

"I mean that people do change and grow when they go away to school, but they change and grow throughout their lives. When two people are married, they don't stop growing, they are just careful to share and grow together. I'm not saying that I won't change when I leave for school. I am saying that no matter how I change, I will stay faithful to you."

She stared at him as the seconds ticked away. As disbelief turned to shock, and shock turned to trust, she said, "I love you."

Greg's entire face lit up. "I love you, too, and I can't believe how lucky I am!"

Slowly she leaned towards him.

"Oh, no you don't. You'd better stay right over there."

"Why? I trust you."

"Look, I don't trust me, okay? If we're going to make it until we get married, we've got to move real slow."

A memory from some class long ago about how difficult life was for teenage boys flashed through Ashley's mind.

"I'm sorry," she said.

"It's okay," he answered, "Just save it for later. Much later."

He got out of the car to walk her to the door. At that moment, Mary Ann opened the door.

"You're home! Oh, thank goodness! Is Megan all right?"

"Yeah, she's fine. Is Dad up, too?"

"Of course. You know him! He wasn't about to go to bed until his baby was home safely."

"I thought he worked nights," said Greg.

"He does," Mary Ann replied, "but they do give him a day off occasionally."

The fact that it was Saturday night struck Greg, and he chuckled at his own thoughtlessness. "Of course they do. I guess I wasn't thinking."

Mary Ann looked Greg in the eye and innocently said, "Oh, you were thinking! It was just about something other than my James."

As both Greg and Ashley blushed red, a very large James O'Connor stepped up behind his wife. Greg was a tall young man, but he was at least two inches shorter than this man, and

Mr. O'Connor outweighed him by more than fifty pounds.

Greg couldn't stop himself from staring, and James O'Connor let out a huge laugh.

"What's the matter, young man?" he teased. "Haven't you ever seen a black Irishman before?"

Without hesitating, Greg threw back, "I don't often meet anyone I could hide behind!"

James O'Connor's laugh roared through the night.

"Good grief, James! You'll wake the neighbors!" said Mary Ann. "Why don't you come in for a minute, Greg?"

"I should be getting home," he said.

"Of course you should!" roared James. "But if ten minutes won't really matter to your parents, I'd love to have you stay. I've been waiting to meet you for some time, now!"

Greg thought of all the times he had stayed out late in the past. His parents trusted him, and this year had given him no curfew.

"I guess ten minutes wouldn't make them worry," he said, but he wasn't so sure he was up to spending ten minutes with this man. In fact, he was pretty sure of it.

Chapter Seventeen

All four of them sat down in the living room. There was one light on the ceiling, doing its best to light the entire room. Two unlit lamps sat on end tables that were purchased at garage sales, and the couch and three chairs looked as if they might have been found in a similar way.

Sitting next to her husband on the couch, Mary Ann O'Connor appeared very small indeed. Her blond hair had some gray in it, contrasting sharply with her husband's brown eyes and hair. They were complete opposites physically, but somehow they looked perfectly matched...and perfectly content with each other.

"So how did the play go tonight?" asked Mary Ann.

"It went fine!" answered Ashley with a little too much enthusiasm. "Megan was wonderful as usual."

"That girl really has talent!" said James. Then turning to Greg, he added, "They actually let me off last night to go see it!" And again, his laughter filled the air.

Greg was not often at a loss for words, but James O'Connor was not like any man he had ever met before. Ever. He seemed like a character out of some movie with a personality as big as his body and his laugh. "Tell me, Greg, how did a young basketball star get interested in drama?"

"How did you know I play basketball?" asked Greg.

"I do know how to read the papers, you know," James answered, smiling. He knew the effect he was having on Greg. He had the same effect on a lot of people, but this time he was playing it to the hilt.

Finally Ashley said, "Oh, Dad, stop it! He knows you read!"

With a hearty laugh, James apologized. "I'm sorry, Greg. You just seemed so hypnotized by seeing me for the first time, I thought I'd get a little extra mileage out of it. "

Greg answered, "I'm sorry, too. I usually meet people fairly well."

"I don't doubt it." By now, James' voice was in a more normal range of volume, and Greg began to see the sensitive side of this huge man.

"I used to play a lot of basketball myself," continued James. "A little football, too. I guess that's one reason I always read the sports page."

Ashley beamed with pride. "He even played college football for awhile," she said.

"Really?" asked Greg.

"Really," James put in, again punctuating his speech with his deep laugh. "I only played for two years, though. Blew out my knee, and that was that."

"That's a tough break!" said Greg.

James shrugged. "It happens. Sometimes God goes to great lengths to steer us in the right direction. If I hadn't blown out my knee, I wouldn't have met Mary Ann. I'll take her over football any day!"

"Oh, James! That's enough!"

"Were you working in the hospital or something, Mrs. O'Connor?" asked Greg.

"I was volunteering. You know, some people in hospitals have all sorts of family members around. But there are lots of others who have days go by when no one comes at all. I just couldn't stand it!"

Mr. O'Connor took up the story. "The college I was going to was 400 miles from my home town. There was no way my folks could come up. Well, that's not fair. They did come up when I had the surgery, but they couldn't stay."

"Did you finish college then?" asked Greg.

"No. No, I didn't. The only way I could afford to go was the football scholarship I had. It didn't make any sense for the college to keep paying for my education when I couldn't play any more. I have no regrets, though," he added, seeing the pity on Greg's face. "They paid for all of my medical treatments, including physical therapy. I couldn't complain about that!"

With a thoughtful look on his face, Greg said, "I think a lot of people I know would complain a great deal."

"I pray every day that God will help me do what He wants me to do," said James. "If it's not what I would have chosen, it's my job to accept it with grace. How can I ask God to give me what I want instead of what He wants for me?"

"You make it sound simple."

"Oh, it's never simple. I'm not that good yet," laughed James.

"I hate to interrupt this," said Ashley. "But I think your ten minutes are up, Greg. Should you be getting home?"

"Yeah. I guess I'd better." And he stood up to go.

"Okay," said James, "but please let me tell you one more

thing."

"Sure," said Greg as he sat back down.

"When you first saw me," explained James, "I made a remark about being a black Irishman."

Greg nodded, so James continued, "I feel very proud of my heritage, and I want you to know rather than trying to guess.

"My grandfather was a true Irishman, red hair, freckles, the whole nine yards. When he met my grandmother for the first time, I think he fell in love with her right then and there."

"She was beautiful!" sighed Ashley. "I wish I looked like her!"

Smiling at his daughter, James said, "She could sing like a bird! But she didn't want anything to do with Grandpa until he finally convinced her that his intentions were honorable. Of course, their wedding was just the beginning of their troubles. Neither blacks nor whites would accept them. They led lonely lives as far as other people were concerned, but they kept each other from feeling lonely. It wasn't until 1953 that they found a group who accepted them with open arms."

"I'll bet that it was the Bahá'í s," put in Greg.

"And you would be right!" chuckled James, his face beaming both at Greg for his insight, and at Ashley for obviously telling him about the Faith. "Faith is everything. A blown out knee is nothing."

"I have a long ways to go," mused Greg. "But now I think I understand at least one thing that attracted me to your daughter."

Ashley held her breath. She had no idea what he was going to say.

"Her faith shines through every day," he said. "She often makes comments about not being pretty enough, but how could any other face look beautiful next to one that radiates like hers?"

Tears clouded Ashley's eyes. No one had ever said anything so amazing about her before. But James' reaction was not so quiet. He crossed the room in only three steps and grabbed Greg's hand, shaking it enthusiastically.

"I couldn't have said it better myself!" he said. And his roaring laughter reverberated through the room until the light on the ceiling shook.

Chapter Eighteen

As Ashley, Brittany, and Megan shuffled into Bahá'í school the next morning, Mr. Jameson called out, "So how was your week? Did students notice you dressing up?"

All three girls burst out laughing. Had it really only been a week since the class had decided to dress up to attract attention to the Faith?

"It's been more like a month!" said Megan.

"That bad?" asked Mr. Jameson.

Megan paused for a moment. "No, not that bad. That *eventful* I think would be more accurate."

"Well, if one of the events put you and Ashley back on speaking terms, it certainly wasn't bad," commented Mr. Jameson.

"Oh," clarified Megan, "We're better than just speaking terms. I finally wised up."

"O-o-o! That sounds interesting!" said Jim, as he sauntered in behind the girls.

"Now, now, Jim," Megan teased. "Brittany has the best story, so you'll have to wait for mine. I think we should start with hers."

Brittany was used to volunteering herself, but she couldn't remember anyone saying they wanted her to be first. As they all sat down, she said, "I don't think my story is any better than anyone else's, really. But I did get to teach the Faith as a result of dressing up this week."

"Really?" asked Mr. Jameson. "That's great! Let's hear the details!"

So Brittany described to the class about answering Ryoko's questions on Tuesday, and how that led to lunch together on Wednesday.

"Her own faith is very strong," said Brittany, "so I don't know that she'd be interested in becoming a Bahá'í, but still, I think we have someone else in the school who knows a little about it and respects it."

"That's tremendous, Brittany! But remember that you have the responsibility to share the Faith. Whether Ryoko is interested in becoming a Bahá'í is between her and Bahá'u'lláh."

"That's true," said Jim, "but on the other hand, the really good teachers at school not only give you information, but inspire you to want to learn more. If we're going to be good teachers, our words and deeds should make people want to know more and more about the Faith. Then we're keeping the gate open for the entry by troops."

No one said a word, but they all stared at Jim.

After a few moments, he said, "Hey! Give me a break! I get serious sometimes!"

That made everybody laugh.

"You've trained us to not take you seriously," replied Zivar.

"Well said," added Mr. Jameson, "But that's our flaw, not his, I think. Our minds should be open, not cluttered with stereotypes."

"Yeah," said Jim, "us football players can be sensitive guys."

Everyone laughed again, and Anita added, "Don't push it, Jim."

"Well, maybe we should get back on task," said Mr. Jameson. "Does anyone else have a teaching story from this week?"

For the first time that any of them could remember, every hand went up into the air. Eyes widened, and some jaws dropped.

They started around the room, letting each person share their experiences from the week. Many times, as one student would say something, others would chime in saying, "That happened to me, too!"

Anita talked about the two boys would had walked up to her in homeroom Wednesday and said that she was being boring this week. When she asked them what they meant, they had said they liked the sexy clothes she usually wore better.

"The nerve of them!" she sputtered. "They thought I was dressing that way to please them!"

Kavian asked, "Were you?"

"Absolutely not!" she answered. But more quietly, she added, "But it made me think. Expressing myself is one thing, but I just might be a little bit responsible for people's reactions to what I do."

"I think I know what you mean," said Megan. "No one can be responsible for anyone else, ultimately. But the old saying 'actions speak louder than words' is true, I think. If we say Bahá'ís have higher morals than most of society today, but we still act…let's face it. in a sexy way, people who are not Bahá'ís won't have any reason to believe us."

She looked around the room and saw all of her classmates' eyes gazing at her. Their expressions were mixed, but she was good enough at reading them, that she knew she had to continue.

Looking at the floor at first, she said, "I had a bad experience last night. It all turned out all right, I guess, but after I had gone to bed, I did a lot of thinking.

"Part of the reason things got so uncomfortable was because of the way someone interpreted my…signals. I guess I can't put all the blame on him."

"Neither can you put all the blame on yourself," soothed Ashley, and Megan looked up and smiled at her.

"Well, I'll tell you one thing!" said Anita, trying to ease the tension-in the air. "My mother and I fought less this week than we ever have!"

She joined in the laughter of the class. but then added. "I have to admit it was kinda nice."

"So what do we do now?" asked Zivar.

"I don't have an answer to that," replied Mr. Jameson. "I think the entire class made a wise decision last week. Let's keep up with the consultation and figure it out together."

"I'll say one thing," said Megan.

"Only one?" teased Jim.

After shooting him a dramatic look of aloof indignation, she continued, "I couldn't have gotten through everything that happened this week without having Ashley to talk to."

Ashley turned crimson, but Megan did not stop there. "If we start trying to live the Bahá'í life not quietly but loudly like we did this week, it's going to be rough. I think the first thing we should do is type out a sheet with all of our addresses and phone numbers on it. Then if anyone is having a tough time, they can call someone in the class."

"Like an advice line?" someone asked.

"No, not really. Just to have someone to talk to who also believes we're doing the right thing, not just being stupid."

"I'd be willing to type it," said Brittany. "My mom has a copier at her office, and we could make copies for everyone."

Mr. Jameson quickly tried to hide his initial surprise. "That would be very kind of you, Brittany."

"Yeah," agreed Jim. "What's the deal?"

The room exploded with comments chastising Jim for his cruel remark.

"Gosh! I'm sorry!" he exclaimed. "I was just teasing."

"Some teasing is funny," answered Zivar. "Some is just plain mean."

"I agree," said Mr. Jameson. "And as much as we hear it all on television and movies, we have to limit ourselves to just the teasing that's funny."

"How am I supposed to know?" asked Jim.

Mr. Jameson looked him in the eye. "You're a very intelligent young man, Jim. I think you know the difference. If you don't, maybe you shouldn't tease at all."

"I wouldn't have anything else to say!"

"Now that's funny!" cried Anita as the entire class burst into laughter.

Jim only replied, "Thanks a lot."

"I have an idea for you," said Megan.

"What makes me think I don't want to hear it?"

She ignored him. "Just imagine that Abdu'l-Bahá is standing next to you all the time. He had a great sense of humor. Would He think that what you were going to say was funny?"

"You gotta be kidding!"

"He's right, Megan," added Zivar. "That would be weird to think of having Abdu'l-Bahá stand beside you all the time."

"As a very wise person once said to me, 'What secrets do you have from God?'"

A hush fell over the class, as she had expected it to.

"Yeah, that was my first reaction, too. But I think it's supposed to be more for comfort and strength than some doomsday squad of angels following you around to write down all your mistakes. One thing's for certain, though. Being a Bahá'í has never been easy, but in these times, it's even harder. Remember Shoghi Effendi said we would have mental tests instead of physical ones like being tortured. I think this is what he was talking about."

"Then that makes it even more important for us to help each other," added Zivar.

"It's like we're warriors," said Kavian.

"More like 'peaciors,'" laughed Brittany.

"Out to save the world!" cried Jim dramatically as he stood up and stretched one arm toward the ceiling.

"Now, that might have been funny," said Mr. Jameson, "if it weren't true."

"What?!"

"Bahá'ís are the ones who are capable of breathing life into the dead spirits of humanity by sharing the teachings of Bahá'u'lláh. And not only that, it has been said more than once that the Youth shall lead the way."

"Whoa…"

As Jim sat back down, the rest of the class was quiet.

"Don't worry! God has said He will never give a soul more than it can bear. And if someone rises to teach the Faith, they will have the heavenly host there to help them."

"But," said Anita, "we are always spending our time getting

ready for something. Getting ready for a test, getting ready for college, thinking about what we're going to do when we grow up. What you're saying is that this is something we're supposed to do now, right?"

"Definitely."

"But look what an effect we had just this week!" recalled Ashley. "We can do it!"

The bell rang that signaled the end of Bahá'í school for that week. Students looked at each other frantically.

"What are we supposed to do?" asked someone.

"It's too late," said Brittany. And as several kids looking at her in shock, she clarified, "It's too late to make a plan for this week, like we did last week. How 'bout if we dress nicely again, maybe not dresses and ties, but look nice? Then we could all work on generating teaching ideas to share with the class next week. I could have the list of names done by then. Who has the sheet Mr. Jameson passed around?"

"Here it is!" said Zivar.

"Okay, thanks. What do you all think?"

Jim stood up. "In all seriousness, Brittany, I think that's a great idea. You do have good ideas, and I'm really sorry for what I said earlier."

This time, it was Brittany's turn to blush.

"Thanks…And it's forgotten."

Ashley put her arm around Brittany's shoulders. Not really knowing why, Megan did the same from the other side.

"You're parents are waiting, and there's a lot of work to do! Get out of here!" laughed Mr. Jameson.

As the students left, he took a moment to sit down before he packed up all of his books.

"Thank you, Bahá'u'lláh, for sending me such good kids," he said out loud. "I think Your Faith is in good hands." Then he laughed at himself. "As if You didn't know!" he added, and he began filling the boxes with his books so he could carry them out to his car.

Printed in the United States
53560LVS00007B/7-15

9 781424 116232